For my family

Praise for The Race

'Not your typical happily ever after,
Roy has written a wonderfully relatable
and inclusive tale, where all are welcome,
and the beauty of sport brings everyone
together in the end.

There are life lessons to be learned
in this inspiring story with
friendship at its heart.'

SHAUNAGH BROWN
International Rugby Player and Former
Commonwealth Games Athlete

'An original, immensely readable take on the
Eric Liddell story for the 21st century.'

SALLY MAGNUSSON

'A very interesting, relatable and
enjoyable read that brings the memory of
Eric Liddell to life.'

ALLAN WELLS MBE
Olympic Gold Medallist

This is what it feels like when I'm running.
When I'm running fast.
It feels like the world has faded away.
Like I'm on my own, even though I know other
runners are there, hot on my heels.
It feels like I'm ready for lift off.
Running flat out but somehow accelerating as well.

When I'm running all my worries disappear and I
concentrate on just two things: the race and myself.
Not what I've done or what I'm going to do,
what I think or even what I feel,
but the real me that appears when I'm running.
I am the arms that are pumping.
The legs that are striding out.
The breath that is pulsing.
When I'm running I don't have a body: I am my body.
This is what it feels like when I'm running.
When I'm running fast, I feel free.

1

Lili

It was Wednesday afternoon and Tom was being annoying.

Tom is annoying most days but that afternoon he was being *really* annoying. I think it's because he was bored. We were in school, which was kind of OK, and we should have been having Sport, but it was pouring with rain, so we had to stay inside.

I think we should have gone out anyway but the teachers said it wasn't safe, which seemed odd because we run around at break whether it's raining or not. The teachers aren't worried then and no one ever gets hurt. Well, not often anyway. And what does it matter if we do get wet? Our skin's waterproof. That's what my Gran says and she's pretty much always right.

So, it was raining and we were cooped up in a classroom, learning about the history of the Olympics when we could have been outside doing actual sport. That's why Tom was being annoying.

'Where did China come in the medal table at the Rio Olympics, Miss?' he called out.

The problem with Tom is that he's actually pretty clever. He's annoying, of course, but he's also smart. I hate to admit it but it's true. He *knew* where China came in the medal table. That's why he was asking.

'Good question, Tom,' Miss Scattergood said. 'I can't quite remember off the top of my head but let's check, shall we?'

I like Miss Scattergood, I really do. She actually listens to what we say and she's got a great collection of purple glasses, but she is a teacher and teachers have a very funny way of speaking. Every question's a "good question" and "let's check, shall we" really means "I'll google it." If I ever become a teacher I'm going to speak normally.

I sat back in my chair and waited for Miss Scattergood to work out how to get connected on the school laptop. I avoided Tom's eye but there was no escaping him really. In every lesson there was always a vague sense that Tom was there, that Tom had been there, or that he was about to appear.

The maps of the world that we'd made last term were a case in point. The purpose of the exercise had been to show that there are different ways of presenting a 3D world in 2D form, but Tom had taken the opportunity to cause mischief as usual. Sophie and Rachel had drawn an enormous Greenland, like the one Miss Scattergood showed us on her Mercator map. Andy and Todd had added a super-large India and my contribution was to put China slap bang in the middle, just like Chinese map-makers used to do. And why not? Why shouldn't China (or India or Greenland, for that matter) be in the centre?

But Tom couldn't cope with China in the middle of the world, so he carefully cut round it so that when Miss Scattergood picked up the map to show the class, China promptly fell to the floor. Tom and his idiotic friends thought this was hilarious. We stuck it back together afterwards but it was never quite the same again.

'Oh, here it is,' Miss Scattergood announced, interrupting my thoughts. 'They came third.'

'And who came second, Miss?' Tom asked. He's so predictable.

Miss Scattergood checked her screen.

'Well, it was Great Britain. That's good, isn't it?'

'You'd think the Chinese would've done better than third, wouldn't you?' he said, half turning so I could see the snarky look on his face. 'There are so many of them.'

Snarky is a good word. It means cranky or cutting. My Gran taught me what it means. She said it might come in useful. She said it's a word teachers should use more often, especially when they're talking about Tom.

'I think China did very well, Tom. And so did Team GB. They both did very, very well.'

'But China didn't do well, did they, Miss?' Tom

insisted. 'We beat them. And that's what sport's all about, isn't it, Miss? Not being a loser.'

'Sport,' Miss Scattergood said, changing her tone of voice and piercing him with a steely look now that she'd worked out what he was up to, 'is all about taking part. So let's get on with the lesson.'

Actually, I wasn't bothered that Britain got more golds than China because I'm Chinese and British. That means I get to support two teams at the Olympics. Britain won 27 gold medals and China won 26. That means my teams won 53 gold medals, which put them in first place. The USA only got 46, so they've got a lot of catching up to do.

In fact, we did even better than that because my family also supports Kazakhstan. My sister, Alice, is Kazakh and British, you see, and she doesn't like to be left out. And Kazakhstan won three gold medals, which took our grand total to 56. I tried to explain this to Tom one day when he was going on and on, but he didn't get it.

He doesn't care: that's why he didn't get it.

But maybe you don't get it either. Our family's not exactly run of the mill, I guess, so I'd better explain. Dad was born in Newcastle but his ancestors came over to Britain with the Normans a thousand years ago (that's why we've got a funny surname that no one can spell —DeLisle) and Mum was born in Glasgow. So I'm English and Scottish. But I'm also Chinese because they adopted me in China when I was eighteen months old.

Not that I can remember, but I've seen the pictures. And then, when I was seven, they adopted my sister from Kazakhstan. I can remember that all right. It was wild. We spent weeks going back and forth to Kaz, staying in a really nice hotel and visiting the orphanage. We had all sorts of funny food as well, string cheese and halva, which is a sort of sweet sunflower paste, and stuff like that. It was really good. And then Alice came home with us and I had a little sister at last.

We're a real League of Nations my Gran says. Which I thought was something to do with sport but apparently it's something to do with history. Anyway, what she means is that we've got lots of different nationalities in our family.

Which is great when it comes to the Olympics.

In fact it's even better than I first thought. I found out a few months ago that my Uncle was born in Greece and they won three golds at Rio. I thought I'd add them to our list as that would have taken us to 59, but Dad said I was getting carried away, and he's probably right because I do sometimes get carried away. Not that I mind. If I get carried away then I get things done.

But try telling Tom any of that and all you get is a snarky comment. Not that I care what Tom says. I'm proud of being Chinese and I'm proud of being British too. Unfortunately some people find it hard to get their heads round that simply because I don't look like my

Mum and Dad. They want to put me in a neat box, stick a label on the front and hope I don't protest. The problem is I don't fit into most boxes and most labels don't stick, so I confuse people.

'The thing is that China just don't have the same track record as us,' Tom added, because he was really trying to wind me up. 'They're still trying to catch up.'

Miss Scattergood sighed and tried not to catch my eye. I kept quiet because what's the point? I knew that in 2008 China got more gold medals than anyone else and I knew that in Rio China won more medals overall than Britain. But Tom isn't really interested in facts. He just likes to be annoying.

'I think you'll find that China have been doing very well in the Olympics for a very long time, Thomas,' she said, trying to close down the conversation.

'Really?' Tom said, scowling. He hates being called Thomas. 'So when did they win their first gold?'

'Well, let's check shall we?' Miss Scattergood said, turning back to her computer.

While she searched, Tom turned round and grinned in triumph. He'd obviously done his research. He thought he'd got one over on me.

'Oh,' said Miss Scattergood, looking up, 'that's not what I expected.'

Tom turned back. Maybe I was imagining it but I thought he looked a bit worried.

'When was it?' he asked.

Whatever it was she'd discovered, Miss Scattergood was obviously enjoying it because she was smiling away to herself.

'When was it?' Tom repeated.

Miss Scattergood looked up and beamed at him. '1924,' she said.

'That's not right,' Tom blurted out.

'Oh yes it is, Tom. 1924. In the 400 metres. A man called Eric Liddell blew the opposition away.' Then she turned to me. 'I think we could have some fun with this, Lili. I really do.'

2

Lili

'She's got to be joking,' Tom muttered loudly enough for me to hear, as we filed out of class. 'Eric! That's not a Chinese name.'

'Since when were you an expert in Chinese names?' Sophie asked. Sophie is my best friend and more assertive than me when dealing with boys.

I nudged her to keep quiet. She was only trying to be helpful but sometimes you've got to pick your battles.

'Since when were you an expert in anything?' Tom replied. 'Eric's clearly not a Chinese name. Scatterbrain's got it wrong again. Just what you'd expect.'

I took Sophie by the elbow and tried to steer her away, but I could see her hackles rising. To be perfectly honest, I don't really know what hackles are or how they rise, but I definitely knew that Sophie's were.

'You're so arrogant, Tom, you really are,' she said, stepping in front of him as he was about to walk off. 'Lots of Chinese people have both western and Chinese names.'

As she waited for him to comment, Sophie folded her

arms and refused to move. She could be as stubborn as him when she thought she was in the right. Tariq and Andy, Tom's sidekicks, edged forward, sensing that they might be called into action but Tom had no intention of resorting to physical force.

'*I tell you what,*' he said. '*Let's check, shall we?*'

His impression of Miss Scattergood was irritatingly good. He grinned at Sophie but I could see that he was half looking at me. Pulling his phone from his jacket pocket, he flicked it on and sidled away from the door.

'If any of the teachers catch you with that, you're going to be in big trouble,' Sophie said.

'Like they're going to notice,' Tom replied, not lifting his eyes from the screen. 'Okey-dokey, what have we got here? Eric. Olympics. Here it is. *Eric Liddell, who was known as the Flying Scotsman, was a student at Edinburgh University when he won gold at the 1924 Olympic Games.* So not Chinese then. Scottish. Which the last time I looked wasn't part of China. Or, if I have to spell it out for your little sprinter friend, I was right and Scatterbrain was wrong. As usual. See ya.'

He could be really obnoxious when he put his mind to it and he put his mind to it quite a lot.

'Come on,' I said, pulling Sophie away. 'We've got Geography to get to and I don't want to be late because of Tom.'

Sophie clenched and unclenched her fists.

'He's such a little…'

I gave her another tug and this time she came. Even so, I could tell that she was brooding all the way through the lesson. At least, she was brooding until Mr Smith nipped out to get some paper. Unable to wait any longer, she got her phone out and started searching. Unfortunately Mr Smith wasn't gone long. Just as she let out a low whistle of triumph, he walked back in, saw her on her phone, confiscated it, put her in detention, and carried on teaching as if he hadn't disappeared from our lesson in the first place. It didn't seem fair.

I didn't really concentrate for the rest of Geography. I did what Tariq and Andy do most of the time: I stared out of the window. And when I'd finished staring out of the window I stared blankly at the walls. It wasn't great but it was better than listening to Mr Smith drone on.

We have 'inspirational' posters all over our walls. The first woman to win a Nobel Prize; the first Welshman to climb Mount Everest; the first child to get a record deal: you know the sort of thing. Then, when we got back after the summer break, we found that a new lot had gone up. Famous people. Or people the teachers thought were famous. There was some businessman I'd never heard of in Social Sciences and a Greek guy I'd never heard of in Maths, but my favourite one was in Religious Studies. They could have chosen Mother Teresa, Martin Luther King, or the Dalai Lama, but instead they went for some philosopher called Elizabeth Anscombe. What I really liked about her was that she was wearing her name badge upside down.

The poster on the wall in Geography wasn't quite as good as that but it was still pretty funny. It was an old picture of map-man Mercator, wearing a big hat and a big beard. He looked a bit odd to be perfectly honest. Anyway, the reason I mention it is because I spent most of the lesson staring at that uninspirational 'inspirational' picture, coming round only when Mr Smith announced the end of the lesson. I still have no idea what he had been talking about.

'I'll see you at training,' Sophie whispered as we packed our bags. 'If old Smithy doesn't keep me back too long.'

She hesitated.

'Or unless training's off. It's still chucking it down out there.'

Then she caught my eye and laughed.

'OK, OK! So you'll be there anyway, whether it's cancelled or not. I knew that really.'

I gave her a big smile and then I smiled at Mr Smith too because it looked like he was going to comment. He hesitated and then walked off because smiling at teachers usually confuses them. Smiling is my secret weapon. I know it doesn't seem like much of a secret weapon but, believe you me, it works. I'll try to explain.

Becoming a great runner is all about training properly. And having some sort of natural talent, I guess. But mainly it's about training. And to train properly you've got to be disciplined. You've got to keep at it. You've got to train when your competitors can't face it. And that means going out in all weathers. I go running in sun and rain, in wind and snow. If it's cold and dark I get up and go out anyway. If it's raining sideways, I still drag myself out through the front door and do my usual circuit. I have to keep going because taking a break for bad weather means I'll slip behind my competitors.

But here's the tricky thing. Getting up when the weather is being very British isn't much fun. I'm just an ordinary girl. I hate bad weather as much as anyone else. So what do I do when it's hurling down rain? I fix a smile on my face and *decide* that I'm going to enjoy it. And if I decide to smile and enjoy myself then I really do enjoy myself. It's like jumping into a cold swimming pool. It's terrible for a couple of seconds but then you don't even remember that it was cold once you get moving.

I know that my rivals are probably sheltering inside if it's terrible weather. Which means I'm getting fitter than them. And if I'm fitter I'm faster. Which is what it's all about. So there was no way I was going to hang about inside just because it was chucking it down. If training was on, I'd train with the rest of the school squad. If it wasn't, I'd train on my own. That was how I'd got to be the district champion. That's how I'd got into the regional squad. That's how I'd qualified for the Nationals.

So straight after school, I rushed off to training and was halfway through a series of circuits when Sophie eventually appeared. She had a grin on her face.

'How was detention?' I shouted as she cut across the long jump area.

'Pointless,' she shouted back. 'But I did manage to find out a bit more when Smithy went off to make himself a coffee.'

Sophie was nothing if not daring. Most people who are in detention for checking their phone during lessons don't start googling under the desk.

'Tom was half right,' she admitted.

'Oh great,' I said ironically.

'But so was Miss Scattergood. Eric Liddell was born in China but his parents were Scottish and he competed for Britain at the 1924 Olympics. It's all in some movie apparently. *Chariots with Fire*, or something like that. Anyway, he was supposed to be running in the 100 metres but because the heats were run on a Sunday he refused to run, so he switched to the 400 metres and that wasn't really his distance. But he didn't have much choice if he didn't want to run on a Sunday. And it all got really tense, especially as he went flat out over the first 100 metres, which isn't how you're supposed to run the 400, but somehow he hung on and won. In fact, he did more than hang on, he broke the world record.'

'I don't get it,' I said. 'Why didn't he want to run on a Sunday?'

'Because he was religious. His Mum and Dad were missionaries in China and they believed that you shouldn't play sport or do any work on Sundays.'

'But running isn't …'

'Look, that's what they believed,' Sophie interrupted. 'Anyway, the point is he refused point blank to run in the 100 metres, which he was favourite for, and competed in the 400 metres instead, even though no one thought he stood a snowball in hell's chance of winning. And because he was born in China and lived in China, the Chinese have claimed him as their very first Olympic gold medallist, so Miss Scattergood was right.'

I started jogging again as I tried to process what Sophie had said. I couldn't get my head round the fact that Eric Liddell had given up the chance of an Olympic gold just because the heats were run on a Sunday. I mean, I go to Church on Sundays, but then I go running afterwards. And if there's a race on then Mum and Dad arrange for us to go to Church somewhere near the competition. I'm not quite sure how they do it but they always seem to find a way.

And I couldn't quite believe that Eric had been born in China, like me, and competed for Great Britain, like me. I'm not used to hearing about people like me; it seemed too wonderful to be true.

'Look, Sophie, I need to get this straight,' I said, once she was jogging alongside me. 'Are you sure he'd qualified for the 100 metres? Maybe it was nothing to do with it being Sunday.'

Sophie sighed in the same exaggerated way that adults use when they're about to patronise you. Then she stopped running, turned to face me and put her hands on her hips.

'I know it's difficult for you to grasp basic facts, Lili, but you've got to forget about the whole Sunday thing. What you've got to hold onto is that he was born in China. He was China's first gold medallist and you're going to be their 250th. But only if you get on with running round this track and stop standing there with rain pouring off your nose. Got it? Good. Now come on, I'll race you to the finishing line.'

3

Eric
Tianjin, China, 1907

The children were struggling with the heat. They had been wrestling against it all afternoon and now, one by one, they slowly admitted defeat. Three little girls in off-white calico dresses were sitting in the shade of a gingko tree, fanning each other with cheap paper fans. A red-haired boy was pouring water over his head from a standpipe in the corner of the yard and spraying his companions every time they came too close. A slightly older boy was sitting with his back to a great brown Labrador, the two of them panting with exhaustion, their tongues out and sweat rolling down their faces.

The remains of their games lay scattered about the yard. A football half-deflated in the back of a goal, two bamboo hoops on the edge of the pitch, and a wooden top, which a couple of chickens were pecking at.

Though the children had all dropped to the ground, the late afternoon was still full of noise. The sound of a heavy hammer resounded across the compound. Frogs croaked in an unseen pond. Two voices rose in song from the squat building behind the goal. Sometimes in unison, sometimes edging towards harmony, they seemed to reach out towards the children who paid no notice at all to the music swirling round them.

As the children slumped in the shade, a small, white-haired woman shuffled into the light. She looked briefly at each of them, but the one she was looking for wasn't sitting with his back to a dog, or resting with his head in his arms, or standing with one arm on the standpipe. The little boy she wanted was the only one still moving. A bundle of perpetual motion, he was shuttling between the goal and the gingko tree, barefooted in the dust. Sometimes he slid up to the turning place. Sometimes he collided with it full on. Accelerating away with a push of his out-stretched foot, he pivoted off the tree to the goal as though he were being pursued. The old lady smiled affectionately and started to clap her hands in time to his five-year-old strides.

'*Kuai dianr! Kuai dianr!*'

The little boy lifted his head for a moment. Intense and serious, he didn't have time or breath to reply but, pounding his little feet hard into the ground, he tried to pick up the pace. The other children joined in the chant.

'Faster, faster, faster!'

The little boy strained against the heat of the afternoon, determined to force another burst of pace from his little legs. Maybe he would have succeeded but his mother, attracted by the sudden surge of sound from the yard, appeared in the doorway behind the white-haired woman.

'Eric!' she shouted. 'That's enough. It's time to come in now.'

The little boy hesitated and then slowed to a halt. His brother peeled himself away from the standpipe, trotted over to where Eric was standing and tried to lift him up.

'Come on, little 'un,' he said gently.

'Do we have to?' the little boy asked.

'Yes we do.'

'Can I come out again tomorrow?'

His brother hitched him up a little higher.

'No we can't. Not tomorrow.'

'Oh, why not?' Eric whined.

'Because tomorrow's a special day,' his brother explained. 'Remember: just like Ma and Pa said. Tomorrow's a day for the Lord, not a day for running yourself into the dust.'

4

Lili

Assemblies in our school always start with a good old sing-song. We work our way through the same seven or eight hymns over the course of a fortnight and then start all over again. I guess our headmaster doesn't have much faith in our musical ability. Perhaps he's right.

'Hymns?' my dad said, sounding completely unconvinced when I listed them for him one evening. 'Sounds like a bunch of second-rate ditties to me.'

I'm not quite sure what a ditty is but I don't think he was being complimentary. There was one exception though. One hymn which escaped his scorn. One tune he couldn't stop whistling for the rest of the week.

'*Jerusalem*! Ah, now we're talking,' he said. 'A proper, old-fashioned, tub-thumping hymn if ever I heard one. There's no point in holding back with Jerusalem. It's one to bellow.'

And he really can bellow when he puts his mind to it. I know this from bitter experience.

'And another thing,' he added, 'if any of your teachers tell you you can't start a sentence with "and" just quote

Jerusalem at them. One of the most famous poems in the English language and it starts with "and". Completely dodgy theology, of course. He was a great poet, William Blake, but utterly barmy.'

And with that he was off, singing at the top of his voice until Mum threatened to send him to the shed if he didn't stop straightaway.

Anyway today was *Jerusalem* day. I think it must have been our headmaster's favourite too because he gave it such a full-throated rendition that he croaked his way through the rest of the assembly, which kept us all amused.

I can't really remember what the assembly was about. Being nice to each other, I suppose. That's what it normally is.

But the notices did make me sit up and listen for a change. After all the usual stuff about drama rehearsals and walking on the left in corridors, the headmaster told us that he had an important announcement to make.

'In this our anniversary year,' he said, 'I am delighted and honoured to say that a very special guest will be joining us for Sports Day. Very, very special.'

He paused, looked round and then frowned because we weren't exactly sitting on the edge of our seats.

'Yes,' he said, clearing his throat, 'it will be a day never to be forgotten. I am pleased to announce that Her Royal Majesty Queen Elizabeth II is coming to see our school, our Sports Day, all you lot in action.'

He looked round again and beamed. It was pretty exciting, I have to admit. I'd never met royalty before. I turned to Sophie but before I could whisper anything, the headmaster started speaking again.

'And to mark Her Majesty's visit, we have decided to shake up the way we run Sports Day,' he added.

Mollie Davis, who was sitting just behind me, leant forward and whispered: 'Free ice cream for us and teachers run the half marathon.'

Miss Baker glared at her, so she sat back in her chair.

'In the spirit of true competition, we have decided to throw open every event to every student. There won't be separate races for girls and boys. Anyone can enter any race. The Queen will see the highest level of competition. The best student will win.'

'That's so unfair,' Mollie said, not even attempting to keep her voice to a whisper.

I wasn't sure if it was fair, but it was certainly a big change. I felt my heart start to pound and tried to work out if it was excitement or nervousness.

I don't want to sound boastful but I've won every school Sports Day I've ever taken part in. I've got long legs and there's something about the way my bones or tendons are structured which means that I'm surprisingly fast for my age. I'm not really sure of the science.

The point is, I'm used to winning, but that's because I usually compete against girls my own age.

If I was going to be up against the boys as well then that changed everything.

I started to work out who the main threats would be. There was Mohammad Siddiq, of course. He won the boys' race last year and I sometimes saw him at district and regional competitions. But he was more of a 400 metres runner so I reckoned I had a chance of seeing him off in the 100 and 200 metres.

Then there was Harry Armstrong. He'd only just joined us from some other school. The rumour was that he'd been expelled. I wasn't too sure about that, but I could tell from playground games of football than he was pretty sharp over short distances.

I reckoned Mohammad and Harry were the ones I really had to worry about.

'You know why they've changed the rules this year?'

It was Mrs Hughes, my form teacher. She was waiting for me as we filed out of the hall.

'No, Miss.'

'It's because of you,' she beamed. 'They thought they'd give you some opposition for a change.'

I looked down, unsure whether I was supposed to be pleased or not.

'Just between ourselves,' Mrs Hughes continued confidentially, 'it might put some of these boys in their place, seeing you collect the gold medal from the Queen. Wipe those really irritating grins off their faces. What do you think?'

There was nothing I could say to that so I simply smiled in reply and muttered something about having to get to my first lesson. Unfortunately when I got there Tom was waiting at the door.

Somehow I'd forgotten about Tom. Tom wasn't a sprinter because *running wasn't a real sport*, as he never tired of telling me. Real athletes didn't prance about on the track. They played proper games like rugby. Like he did. That's what he said.

So I didn't often get to see him run. I knew he went training on Tuesdays and Thursdays after school. I knew he played rugby for the school on Saturday mornings and for his club on Saturday afternoons (because he never stopped boasting about it). But I'd forgotten that he was a winger. Which meant that he must be quick.

'Oi, Lee Lee.' He knows my name isn't pronounced like that but he always says it that way to annoy me. 'Looks like you're in trouble now, eh? It's not going to be your usual stroll in the park.'

I walked to my desk and tried to ignore him, but he wasn't going to let it go.

'Reckon Mo's going to have you for breakfast. And Harry. Chances are you're not even going to come third.'

He turned and grinned at one of his sidekicks, Adam Carter, who had so much trouble stringing a sentence together that he usually let Tom do it for him.

'In fact, you're not. Know why? Cos I've decided I'm going to teach you what real runners look like. For this year only I'm going to swap my rugby boots for running spikes and leave you for dust.'

He spun on his heel and banged fists with Adam. I sat down and tried not to feel upset.

What most people don't appreciate about runners is that we get on really well with each other. Most weekends I'm travelling up and down the country to some athletics meet or other, so I spend more time with my running friends than I do with my school friends. I just don't have time to do all the usual stuff, like parties and shopping trips. On Monday mornings, when Mollie and Aisha and the others get talking about what they've been up to at the weekend, I feel cut off from the lives they lead, but it doesn't bother me. I don't feel like I'm missing out because I've usually spent the weekend somewhere new, catching up with my running friends and pushing myself to do my best. I haven't got time to waste hanging around Top Shop.

And I haven't got time to waste on disliking my competitors either. I get on really well with most of them and it's no use pretending otherwise. Mrs Hughes once asked me how I could bear to beat them if they were my friends, but the truth is I couldn't imagine beating them if they weren't my friends. That would feel cruel.

But now Tom had reared his ugly head, which meant

that I had a problem.

'What's wrong, Lili?' Dad asked when I got home. 'You're looking a bit down in the dumps.'

'Oh, it's nothing. Just school,' I said. There are some problems it's just too difficult to explain.

At least I thought it was too difficult to explain, but then I walked into the sitting room and found Gran sitting there, a big grin on her face.

'Gran, what are you doing here?' I yelled, throwing myself at her.

'I've come for a little holiday,' she said, once she'd pulled herself free from my hug.

Gran's in her 90s now and isn't so good on her feet, which is bad and good news. Bad because she clearly finds it painful to walk anything more than short distances, but good because she now spends more time with us.

'What's all this about you being down in the dumps? You're usually such a cheery little soul.'

I don't know what it is about Gran but it's easy to tell her stuff. She just lets me splurge it all out without interrupting and then, when I've finished, she doesn't say much in response. This time was no different. Once I'd finished telling her about the Queen and complaining about Tom, she leant back in her armchair, took another sip of stone-cold tea and looked thoughtful.

'Well it seems pretty clear to me,' she said eventually.

'You've just got to out-nice him.'

'You're going to have to explain that one to me, Gran,' I replied.

'You know what Harry Truman said? No, of course you don't because you don't know who Harry Truman was, do you?'

I shook my head.

'Well, he was President of the USA and a very clever man, though a bit of a scoundrel. Anyway, what he said was that if you can't convince them you've got to confuse them.'

That took a bit of getting my head around.

'I'm not sure I see what that's got to do with Tom, Gran,' I said.

'He's being unpleasant and he's expecting you to be unpleasant back, so you'll have to confuse him by being as nice as pie. That'll throw him. He won't be used to someone being nice to him *and* trying to beat him at the same time. People like Tom don't realise that being nice isn't a sign of weakness but a sign of strength. And when I say you've got to out-nice him, I mean it. He's going to have one heck of a surprise when it comes to Sports Day.'

She settled back into her chair with a look of triumph on her face while I tried to work out whether what she'd said was brilliant or bonkers. As it was Gran, I gave her the benefit of the doubt.

'I'm looking forward to it, I really am,' she continued.

'I think I'll buy myself a nice new hat for the occasion. After all it isn't everyday you see the Queen.'

She looked so happy I didn't really have any choice but to give her my biggest smile and nod in agreement.

'OK, Gran,' I said, 'I'll give it a go.'

'Great! Game on! That's what you youngsters say, isn't it? No, don't answer that. Tell me about your training schedule instead and then I'll tell you how you can improve that too.'

5

Eric
The Indian Ocean, 1908

'Is this Scotland?'

Mary Liddell tried not to smile, even though she couldn't imagine anywhere less like Dalwhinnie where she had grown up. She was standing with her youngest son at the railings of *The Princess Alice*, looking out across the Indian Ocean. Soon the bright lights of Calcutta would cut through the early morning gloom and, shortly after that, the sound of its 900,000 inhabitants would race towards them across the waters.

'No, we've a little way to go until we reach Scotland,' she replied, her Highland accent undimmed through nine years of service in China. First Ch'ao Yang then Shanghai then Tientsin. Nine years that now allowed her and her husband the luxury of a year's furlough back home in Scotland.

Once they had got Rob, Eric and Jenny settled into school, there would be time to take the train up to Edinburgh and from there to Inverness. After so many years away from home she was looking forward to home cooking, sea breezes and heather on the glens.

But before that there was a week in India, where James planned to meet old colleagues from the London Missionary Society, and she planned to buy fresh fruit. Then it was back onto the boat for the five week journey to Britain via the Suez Canal. Mary sighed. She had only just found her sea-legs and the prospect of another bout of sea-sickness depressed her.

'How far?' Eric asked, breaking into her daydream.

'What's that, my love?'

'How far to Scotland? Will we be there tomorrow?'

Mary suppressed a smile.

'No, not tomorrow and not the next day either. So you need to go and find something to keep you occupied. Why not ask your father if he'd like a little game of chequers?'

As Eric toddled off, Mary turned back to the rail and sighed. She loved China but she still missed home. She still felt Scottish. However long she was away, however far she wandered, Scotland would always be home for her. But where was home for her children, she wondered? Would it be China? Or would they slowly learn to be British now that they were off to school in Eltham? Now that they were being taken away from all they had ever known?

Maybe China would always pull them back. Secretly

that was what she hoped. Or maybe not so secretly. She and James had committed their lives to the great Middle Kingdom, as the Chinese called their country, but China was not a safe place for children. For the time being they were safer in Britain.

But later, when the children completed their schooling, what would they do then? Maybe they would rejoin them in China and serve the Chinese people she had grown to love and respect. That was her fervent hope.

Mary looked back towards the east and thought about all they had left behind: the churches where they had worked for so many years; the house they had gradually transformed into a home; their friends. She was and always would be Scottish but China was where she and the children now belonged. They might have to spend some time back in Britain but she hoped and prayed that one day Eric, Rob and Jenny would rejoin them in the land of their birth, would take up the baton, would pass on the flame.

6

Lili

I began my campaign to out-nice Tom the next day, though I have to say that it wasn't easy. It was raining again for a start, which meant that we were stuck inside when we could have been outside running.

While we waited for Miss Scattergood to get herself organised, I stared at a wall and tried to imagine I was outside. Miss Scattergood's posters didn't exactly help. One of them showed you how to throw a ball and another one how to hold a bat. Sophie once suggested to Miss Scattergood that she put one up that showed you how to breathe, but the irony was lost on her.

'OK, class,' Miss Scattergood piped up at last, 'who can tell me what we were looking at last lesson?'

I decided to keep my head down.

'Lili?'

I sighed. What was the point of keeping your head down if teachers asked you questions anyway?

'Eric Liddell, Miss,' I replied. 'China's first Olympic gold medallist.'

I felt a stirring from one of the desks in front of me.

31

It was Tom.

'Actually, Miss, I did some extra research off my own back and I found out that he was British, Miss. He wasn't running for China when he won his gold medal.'

'Good for you, doing some additional work in your own time. Have a merit point for that. And yes, you're right, he did run for Britain but he was born in China.'

I was tempted to point out that '*off my own bat*' was the phrase, rather than '*off my own back*', and even more tempted to say that flicking on your phone hardly counts as extra research, but I kept quiet and smiled instead.

'So, not for China,' Tom said, just in case I'd missed it.

Refusing to rise to the bait, I smiled at his sneer and watched with delight as an uncertain look crossed his face.

'No, not for China,' Miss Scattergood said, 'but the Chinese regard him as their first gold medallist. He was one of their own.'

'But he wasn't Chinese, Miss,' Tom insisted.

Tariq and Andy sat up. They like a good argument. I shrunk back into my chair because I knew that Miss Scattergood could be as determined as Tom when she put her mind to it.

'He was born in China, Tom, and he lived in China for most of his life. And he died in China too. I think that makes him Chinese, don't you?'

But Tom wasn't having any of it. He was beyond

determined. He was downright stubborn.

'No, Miss, I don't. His parents weren't Chinese.'

'There are plenty of people whose parents were born in one country before moving to another one,' Miss Scattergood countered.

Tom was beginning to get really exasperated now. He was holding onto the side of his chair and pushing himself up as if that would add weight to his point.

'But he was white, Miss!' he said, his voice almost rising to a shout.

Classrooms are never entirely silent. Parents assume they are. Teachers sometimes pretend they are. But they're not. There's always someone talking or coughing or scraping their chair. But when Tom said what he said the room went silent. Realising that he'd gone too far, he subsided into his chair and waited for the inevitable. A low note of anger emerged from the other side of the room. It was Micah Jones whose family was from Ghana and who, unluckily for Tom, was also the tallest and strongest boy in the class.

'What are you saying?' he said in a dangerously quiet voice.

'I'm saying he was British,' Tom replied in a more subdued voice than normal.

'You're saying you have to be white to be British?'

'OK, Micah, thank you. I'll take over from here,' Miss Scattergood intervened. 'I think you might want to retract that statement, Tom.'

Tom looked momentarily confused.

'You might want to apologise,' Miss Scattergood explained, 'and withdraw your comment, which was at best tactless and at worst ...'

She left the sentence dangling. Tom shifted uncomfortably in his chair.

'Yes, Miss. All right, so I wasn't saying you have to be white to be British but ...'

'But what, Tom?' Miss Scattergood asked icily.

Micah looked as if he was going to get out of his chair anyway. Tom looked as if he was going to hide behind his.

'Nothing, Miss.'

'As I thought.' She peered down at him with a grim look on her face. 'Well, in that case maybe we can get on with the lesson?'

Neither Micah nor Tom looked too happy but she carried on anyway.

'As I was saying, Eric Liddell won gold in the 1924 Olympics for Britain, but he is also regarded as China's first Olympic gold medallist. He was a remarkable man at a remarkable Olympic Games, so I thought we'd all do a project about him. That is, you can all do a project about him. Either on your own or in pairs. Your first step is to go onto the internet and do some research, then I want you to report back next lesson with the topic you're going to write about. It could be the 1924 Olympics. It could be just the 400 metres race. Or it could be something else entirely. It's your call. Any questions? No? Good. Well, in that case, as it's still raining you can start your research now. One computer between three and if anyone wants to borrow an iPad I've got a strictly limited supply at the front. OK, let's go.'

I don't know why but Tom turned round and looked straight at me. I guess he was daring me to say something. I simply smiled back.

7

Eric
Eltham College, England 1918

Eric was overawed by the headmaster's study. The leather-clad books, the enormous black chair, the silver fountain pen laid on the headed notepaper. As he shuffled his feet nervously, the headmaster leant forward and examined him.

'So what is it you plan to do with your life, Liddell?' he asked, without any hint of an introduction.

'I believe I am being called to China, sir,' Eric replied.

The headmaster nodded. Eric could tell he was pleased.

'And what do you plan to do in the meantime?'

'I mean to study science at university, sir,' Eric said.

'A worthy notion, though I would have thought medicine more practical. Which university?'

'My father wishes me to study in Edinburgh, sir.'

Mr Robertson sat back in his enormous chair, a slight frown passing over his face.

'I hesitate to gainsay anything your father has

suggested, Liddell. He is a wise and good man in an age when the two are rarely found together. So Edinburgh it will be, to study science perhaps. But do you have no other ambitions?'

Eric hesitated. Ambition was not held in high regard at Eltham College, unless it was ambition on the Lord's behalf.

'I have been given a talent,' he replied slowly, having searched carefully for the correct words, 'and I believe I am meant to exercise it, though I do not yet know to what end.'

Mr Robertson nodded again. He was known and respected as a man of few words.

'I have seen you play, Liddell. It was a fine try you scored last Saturday against St Joseph's. There is much to be said for rugger. It builds character. It teaches fair play and team spirit. If that is your talent then you must use it, as long as your studies do not suffer.'

Eric unfolded his hands and tried to hold the headmaster's gaze.

'I thought I might also join the Athletics Club, sir,' he said.

Mr Robertson leant forward again, picked up his pen and tapped it on the desk.

'The good Lord has given you talent but he has also called you to a task, Liddell, a task no other man can do. I do not know what that task is and nor yet do you. In fact, you may never know it in this lifetime, but, even so, you can be sure that your task has been set down for you. So I ask you: are you sure that you are doing God's will or are you rather indulging your own desires?'

Eric paused a long while to consider his answer, knowing that only an honest response would do, knowing too that Mr Robertson would give a full report of their conversation to his parents. The grandfather clock clicked heavily in the corner. A dog barked distantly. The headmaster's pen continued to tap.

'I do not know, sir,' he said, lowering his eyes, 'but I do know this: God made me fast and nothing God does is without a reason.'

When he looked up again, he saw that Mr Robertson was smiling.

'That is a fine answer, Liddell. Your mother and father would be proud if they could see you now.'

He unscrewed the lid from his pen and began to write.

'You may go now.'

8

Lili

I've always been intrigued by what elite athletes do just before a 100 metres final. Most of them ignore their competitors completely and focus on their own rituals. Some of them strut up and down the track, trying to impose themselves on the field. Others take an age on the starting line, positioning their blocks to the millimetre, stretching and bending in the same way every time, placing their fingers behind the line as if they're about to pick a stray petal from a freshly iced wedding cake.

It wasn't like that with Eric Liddell. From what I've read, he spent more time checking his fellow athletes were OK than he did trying to psych them out. There were no blocks in those days. You dug a hole into the cinder track with a trowel so you had something to push your foot against at the start.

One day one of his competitors forgot his trowel so Eric gave him his without a second thought. Another time he went out of his way to calm an Indian runner's nerves on the starting line when everyone else was ignoring him simply because he was Indian. Eric Liddell didn't have a problem with race. Just as he didn't have a problem with races, not unless they were run on a Sunday anyway.

When Tom turned up to athletics training for the first time he obviously didn't model himself on Eric Liddell. I've never seen anyone our age strut about the track as much as he did that afternoon. Sticking his chest out, he kept eyeballing Harry and Mohammad. Deliberately crossing into my lane, he broke into sudden press-ups and tried to impress me with his manly strength. Or what he reckoned was his manly strength. He obviously didn't realise that I can do press-ups as well as any boy in our year.

'How lovely to see you, Tom,' I said when he crossed into my lane for about the tenth time. 'I'm so glad you could make it today. It's going to be really fun racing against you.'

Then I turned to Billy Battle, my coach, to see how he was reacting to Tom's antics. When Billy saw me looking at him, he glanced over at Tom and rolled his eyes. I couldn't help grinning. Billy's great. He's in his seventies but he's an amazing coach and he's still pretty quick over short distances. In his day he competed for Britain in the high hurdles, so he knows everyone and everyone knows him. More importantly, he knows everything there is to know about athletics. I'm really lucky to have him as a coach.

Anyway, Billy knew exactly what Tom was up to and so he made sure the session suited me rather than Tom. Tom was just itching for a race so Billy did everything but race. We started off with a slow jog round the track. Then we went into a series of slow stretches (which I'm pretty sure were designed to bore Tom so much that he never came back). After that we did loads of sit-ups and press-ups. Out of the corner of my eye I could see Tom grimacing. He was obviously in some pain and it didn't help that I was cruising through Billy's routine. Eventually we got onto actual sprinting but, even then, Billy refused to do what everyone was expecting.

'Right then, team,' he announced in his slightly husky voice. 'Today we're going to work on your starts. Getting a good start is like telling a good joke.' He paused for a moment. 'It's all in the timing.'

I laughed even though I'd heard him say it a hundred times before. Tom just scowled.

'Crazy old has-been,' he muttered under his breath.

Billy, whose hearing was still pretty good, chose to ignore him.

'Let's see what your reflexes are like,' he said. 'When I fire the starting pistol, you're going to push off to the ten metre line and no further. Keep low for the first three strides and then gradually come up to your full height. Sophie, that shouldn't take you long.'

Sophie poked out her tongue at him. She's pretty much

41

the smallest in our year so it's a miracle she can sprint at all. In fact, she's living proof that you can't pigeonhole people. When she first turned up to Athletics Club, Mrs Harvey tried to persuade her to join the long distance runners. Sophie refused to budge and insisted on having at least one go in the sprints. Once was enough. From that day onwards she was a regular member of the sprint squad.

I gave Billy a grateful smile. He knows that starts are one of my strong points. I've got really good reactions and, after hours of drilling, a really good technique too. I've won lots of races I shouldn't have simply because I made a great start and that immediately put the other runners under pressure.

Tom wasn't bad either, I'll give him that. He was unpolished, as you'd expect from a rugby player, but he was pretty quick. Though not as quick as me. We had five gos and each time I got to the ten metre line before he did. He wasn't happy.

'Come on, Billy,' he whined. 'Can't we get onto the real thing now? I want to do the full 100 against the clock and against all this lot too.'

'Hold your horses, young man,' Billy replied. 'We can't run before we can walk.'

'I can run already. I was just wondering when we're actually going to do any at this so-called Athletics Club.'

Billy walked slowly over. He wasn't that much taller

than Tom but Tom still took a step back.

'Look, sonny,' Billy said slowly and deliberately. 'If you want to be part of this club you're very welcome but there are two rules. One, you do as I say. And two, you aren't lippy. Otherwise, there's the changing room.' He pointed over his shoulder. 'I believe rugby practice is on Tuesdays.'

Tom scowled and for a second I thought he was going to answer back but somehow he managed to keep quiet. He must have really, really wanted to beat me at Sports Day.

Billy waited for a moment and then wheeled away, giving me a sly thumbs up as he did so. Gratefully, I raised a thumb in response. He's as tough as old leather is Billy and he's also what Gran calls a 'wily old bird'. He may have left school aged fourteen but he's as smart as they come.

We did some more work on explosive starts and then, ten minutes before the end of the session, Billy surprised us all by announcing that we'd finish with a 100 metres against the clock.

'Sophie, you're up first,' he announced. 'Then Harry, Mohammad, Arthur, Josh, Amelia, Lili and last, but not least, Tom.'

Sophie wasn't too happy about going first but she powered off anyway and clocked quite a decent time, though nothing like as good as Harry's or Mohammad's.

They really flew down the track, which made me nervous for the first time in days. Arthur calmed me down because he was really slow out of the blocks and neither Josh nor Amelia posted great times either. By the time it was my turn, I'd recovered my focus.

'OK, Lili, you're next,' Billy shouted from the other side of the track.

He didn't say anything else but I could still hear his voice in my head as I adjusted my blocks and went through my starting routine. Keep focused on a point ten metres beyond the finishing line. Feel the power in your legs and push through them to your arms when you feel the pistol fire. Don't wait until you hear it. The others will be gone if you do that. Then keep low and gradually rise to your full height. Pump those arms, lift those knees and pound your feet hard into the track. You can do it, Lili. You're good. You're a natural. So keep your head, keep your focus and all will be well.

I have no idea what Tom was doing as I got myself ready. I was completely in my zone. It was only a practice but, as Billy had taught me long ago, you have to treat every practice session as seriously as you would a race.

'On your marks!'

I could feel the coil in my legs, ready to spring.

'Set!'

I took a slow, deep breath in.

'Go, go, go,' Sophie shouted as Billy fired his pistol,

but I was already gone. I got a great start. I knew that it was going to be a quick one from the moment I hit my first full stride and then I was going full pelt down the track, a slight breeze behind me, my eyes focused on that point beyond the 100 metre mark. I was running with the sort of rhythm runners dream about. My legs were pumping, my arms were driving. I was running free and fast and knew, as I dipped at the line, that I had put in a great time.

'Great running, Lili,' Billy shouted from the start line and then he shouted a time. A great time. I was the quickest so far. Which only left Tom.

I wandered back down the track as Tom got ready. He was prowling. It's the only word to describe the way he was moving. He was really unsettled. He was spoiling for action. He was as tense as a hungry predator. And potentially as dangerous. The only question was whether he could channel all that nervous energy into pure speed.

'On your marks!' Billy shouted. 'Get set!'

Tom and the pistol seemed to fire at exactly the same time. He got away from his blocks really well and he had genuine pace. His technique was still a bit ropey— he rolled rather than flew—but he had the sprinter's genuine speed. The only problem was that he was straining. I could see it on his face and even in his arms as he tried to drive himself forward. He dipped way too early as well, which must have lost him a precious few tenths of a second. But, even so, I was worried that he had beaten my time.

'Well run, Tom,' I shouted, determined to keep the niceness going, but I wasn't looking at Tom. I had my eyes fixed on Billy who was staring at his stopwatch as if he couldn't believe his eyes. I felt my heart start pounding almost as much as if I was running. Then Billy gave the stopwatch a shake.

'Darned thing,' he said, loudly enough for us all to hear. 'What a time to stop working!'

Tom, who had jog sprinted back, couldn't believe his ears. 'What do you mean?'

'Sorry, Tom,' Billy said, not looking very apologetic. 'The watch malfunctioned. I don't have a time for you.'

Tom muttered all sorts of stuff that I dare not repeat and then stormed off to the changing rooms. Mohammad, Harry and the others wandered slowly after him. I scooped up my spike bag and was about to go as well when Billy called me over.

'Have a look at this, Lili,' he said. He was holding out the stopwatch.

'It didn't...'

'No, it didn't stop working at all,' he confirmed. 'But he doesn't need to know that.'

I gave him a great big smile.

'Thanks, Billy. I'll see you on Thursday.'

I kept smiling all the way back to the changing rooms

too. I'd beaten Tom by almost half a second and suddenly life seemed really good again.

9

Eric
Paris, January 2nd 1922

Half an hour before the whistle blew, Eric excused himself, walked to the centre of the pitch and looked around. He wanted to savour this moment before the international began. He wanted to take in the size of the stadium, the enormity of the occasion, the responsibility that had been handed to him.

He was making his debut for Scotland against the French. He was part of a new era for Scottish rugby. After the disasters of 1921—defeats against England, France and Ireland—the selectors had made sweeping changes, giving caps to 8 new players, Eric included. Representing his country for the first time, he wanted to make sure he was ready.

'Come on, Liddell,' the head coach shouted. 'Time for sightseeing's over.'

Eric bowed his head, then trotted over to the rest of the team. Leslie Gracie, who had been at school with him, put his arm around his shoulders.

'It'll soon be time to show us your skills, Liddell,' he said.

The next fifteen minutes were spent doing press-ups and short sprints. Then a ball was lobbed onto the field and the team passed it between them. Eric tried to keep his mind on the warm up but it wasn't easy. The stadium at Colombes was used not just for rugby internationals but also for association football and, much more significantly as far as he was concerned, for the forthcoming Olympic Games. Was there any chance he could play rugby for Scotland and sprint for Britain? Was he boosting or ruining his chances by attempting to do both? Was he ready to compete at the highest level in two sports?

He didn't know and the uncertainty unnerved him. Then he pulled himself together. In a few minutes he would be making his debut. He would be playing for his country, his university, his family, and God. He needed to focus on the task at hand.

When the band struck up with the national anthems, his thoughts fell into line. 37,000 spectators were singing their hearts out and he sang with them. He was still a student and nothing he had learned at Edinburgh had prepared him for an occasion like this, but still he sang and when the last note ended he knew that he was ready.

The French flew at them from the very start. The crowd was behind them and they were determined to begin the year with a decisive win. Eric dug in, tackling hard, covering the centres when they were dragged out of position, racing across to the other wing when the French pack poured forward towards the Scottish line. There were precious few opportunities to attack, though he did once swoop on a loose ball, sidestep René Crabos, the French captain, and surge over the halfway line. Looking for support, he found that he was on his own, but in that moment of hesitation the impetus was lost and he was snaffled by the French full back. A couple of minutes later, Crabos broke free, handed off a despairing Scottish defender and lunged over the try line. The French were ahead.

The next ten minutes were desperate. The Scottish were in danger of being overwhelmed by the resurgent French, who were backed vociferously by the partisan crowd. Somehow they held on and then, for the first time since the start of the match, they managed to claw their way back into contention. The breakthrough came when Jock Wemyss, undaunted by the fact that he had lost an eye in the war, charged through the French line before slipping the ball to John Bannerman. With the French drawn into the centre to repel the attack, Bannerman hurled the ball back to Jenny Hume, who spun it wide to Leslie Gracie. Gracie broke the first tackle and then found his fellow centre, Phil Macpherson, who broke through another tackle. Then, just when it looked as if he had carried the ball too far, he whipped it out to Arthur Browning who was powering down the wing. Taking the ball in his stride, he raced clear and dived into the corner for the equalising try. On the opposite wing, Eric raised his arms in celebration and roared his approval.

With the scores level at halftime, the two teams gathered into their huddles and took instructions from their coaches. Eric, hands on hips, knew what was expected of him. He might get only one chance but that split second might mean the difference between victory and defeat.

What neither side anticipated was the downpour that started as the referee blew his whistle. The ball became slippery. Long passes went astray. The already sodden pitch became a mudbath that reminded several players of the trenches. Time and time again the Scots threw themselves at the well-organised French defence. Time and time again they were repelled. Eric ran and tackled with the best of them but not once did he get a chance to do what he did best: run free and fast for the opposition try line. The two teams battled and the crowd still roared, but there was no further score. The match ended in a muddy draw.

In his first international, Eric had neither scored nor won but, as he left the pitch, sodden with rain, he felt content. He had done his bit for team and country. His parents would indeed be proud.

10

Lili

Things were looking up. I'd beaten Tom at training and I was hitting top form just in time for the Regional Championships. That was important because winning at the Regionals meant qualifying for the Nationals. Nothing else mattered for the time being. Not Tom, not the Queen, not Sports Day. On Saturday I was going to get my head down and run.

Sophie hadn't qualified this time so I got to spend time with my other running friends, Frankie and Olivia, who also happen to be my main rivals. We have pretty much nothing in common, Frankie, Olivia and me, apart from running. But running's enough. Not because we talk about it much—we don't—but because we all have the same pattern to our lives. Train, work, train some more and then race. We meet up at the same competitions, read the same running magazines, and buy pretty much the same kit.

But that's all we have in common. Frankie's really posh. She goes to some expensive private school where they have boarders and straw hats and ridiculously short terms. Olivia doesn't even go to school. She's home educated, which means that the only boarders are her brothers and sisters—all five of them—and the only uniform is whatever she pulls out of her wardrobe that morning. And forget the idea of term times, it's all one long holiday for her. That's what I think, though Olivia says it's a bit more complicated than that.

Frankie and Olivia are great but in completely different ways. Frankie's always meeting someone really interesting or someone really famous (or someone really interesting *and* really famous) and Olivia's always got a good story to tell. This time it was all about her tortoise.

'I only turned my back on him for a few seconds and he was gone!' she was saying as I strolled over to the long jump pit to join them.

'Who?' I asked.

'Zeno, my swift-footed tortoise,' she replied.

That's the other thing about Olivia. All her pets (and she's got a lot of pets) have got crazy names. She's got an iguana called Sir Lancelot, a couple of ferrets called Ant and Dec, a dog called Peter Rabbit (for reasons that I've never been able to establish), and a whole bunch of stick insects who are named after characters from Shakespeare's plays.

Oh yes, and a tortoise called Zeno. Zeno was the biggest problem of the lot.

'I put him out in the garden for a few minutes so he

could stretch his legs and then I got distracted by the ferrets. I was trying to give Ant some food but Dec kept muscling in and then he had a little bite at me. Anyway, by the time I'd sorted them out Zeno had scarpered. Don't believe any of that tortoise and the hare stuff. I tell you, when tortoises get the bit between their teeth they really take off. Over short distances they're dynamite.'

I grinned. The story would almost certainly go on for some time and almost certainly end with Olivia and Zeno being safely reunited after a lengthy search. And the whole story would explain why she was late to the meeting. Olivia was always late. One memorable Saturday we were setting up our blocks ready for a race when her parents' car screeched through the car park and right up to the fence. Olivia leaped out, hurdled the fence and somehow sweet talked the starter into letting her compete, even though she hadn't registered and could only find one of her spikes. She still came second.

'And do you know where he was?' she said as I tuned back in.

Frankie shook her head.

'Climbing in through the cat flap!'

'But you haven't got a cat,' I said.

'Exactly. He was just taking advantage.'

I haven't got time to have any pets of my own so I just enjoy them through Olivia. There's never a dull animal moment when she's around. In fact, that's how we first met. Frankie was consoling her after a race so I went over to help in case she was injured, but it turned out she was only upset because one of her stick insects had disappeared that morning.

'But it was Macbeth,' she wailed. 'And he was my favourite!'

Eventually Frankie calmed her down by telling her a long story about how she'd bumped into Prince Harry at a polo match. I can't remember the details but there was something about an ice cream and a new cashmere sweater she'd been given. Anyway, it cheered Olivia up and then, half an hour later, she beat us both in the 200 metres final. We've been friends ever since.

This is how it works at our competitions: I win a heat, then Olivia wins a heat, then Frankie wins a heat. Then we all do well in the semi-finals, which means that it's an all-out sprint for first place in the final. So far, it's 7 wins to me, 6 to Olivia and 4 to Frankie. But it's always close and, just occasionally, someone else comes flying through and surprises the lot of us.

That's what happened this time.

The first heat of the 100 metres went really well. I powered out of the blocks and won 'by a mile,' as Gran announced from her wheelchair when I got back to the stands. It was a really good start to the day but I knew it was only a first step. I still had the 200 heats and the 100 semis to come and then, if everything went to plan, the finals of both races. It was going to be a long day with lots of waiting around, lots of warming up and lots of warming down again.

'Can we go home now?' Alice shouted.

'Not quite yet,' Mum replied. 'Lili's got a few more races to run.'

'But she winned already,' Alice insisted.

I winked at mum and wandered off to catch up with Olivia and Frankie. We chatted about this and that and then we cheered each other on in the different heats. By the time morning tipped into afternoon we had all qualified for both the 100 and 200 metre finals. *So far, so good*, as Gran says every time she lets herself down onto our sofa with a satisfied sigh (sofa so good: geddit?).

The 200 final was first and that went as smoothly as a very smooth smoothie. I got out of the blocks really well, was comfortably ahead of Olivia and Frankie by the time I rounded the bend and then kept powering through until I broke the tape. I was easily first with Olivia second and Frankie third.

But then things started to fall apart.

I was watching the 800 metres when I heard a familiar voice behind me.

'Oi, Lee Lee.'

It was Tom.

I swung round and, rather more sharply than I had intended, asked him what on earth he was doing there.

'There's a big rugby tournament just down the road,' he announced smugly. 'We won it, of course, and I was player of the tournament, so I thought I'd stick my head in here and see what you second-class athletes are up to.'

He's so obnoxious, he really is.

I was about to lay into him when I remembered Gran's advice. I stopped myself, took a deep breath and smiled broadly instead.

'That's very kind of you, Tom,' I said. 'Maybe you can give us some tips on how to improve.'

'Err, yeah, whatever,' Tom replied, looking completely baffled. It was fantastic.

'That's great then,' I said with an even bigger smile. 'I'll see you later. Bye.'

This time Tom couldn't muster any response at all, so I strolled off to see Frankie and Olivia, leaving him to mull over whether to stick around or not.

Unfortunately for us all, he decided to stay. I saw him by the side of the track as I was warming up for the 100 metres final and grimaced, despite my best efforts not to show any sign of irritation when he was around. The thing was, I really needed to concentrate. This final was important. The final is when tenths of seconds matter. The final is the time to put what we've practised all year into operation.

Focusing on the track in front of me, as Billy had taught us, I tried to block out the runners on either side.

I also tried to block out Tom, but that wasn't so easy because he had deliberately positioned himself right in my eye line. Screwing up my eyes, I focused on those first three strides, so that when the gun fired I would surge away from the blocks and run with only Billy's voice in my head as company.

The problem was that the starter held us on the blocks for a really long time. Somehow no one false started, but when he did eventually let us go, I got away really slowly. Either side of me, Frankie and Olivia both started much quicker and so I immediately felt the pressure. I could feel myself straining and by the time I relaxed into my stride it was too late. Olivia stormed through in first place, a new girl we'd never met before burst through from lane one into second place, which left me in third and Frankie in fourth. All I could hear as I crossed the line was Tom's voice cutting across the track.

'Loser!' he shouted, before turning on his heel and swaggering off.

'Don't be upset,' Gran said when I wandered slowly back to see her. 'You still did really well.'

'I'm not upset, Gran,' I explained. 'I'm annoyed with myself. I sort of tensed up and you can't run fast when you're tense.'

'Well, it looked pretty fast to me,' she said. 'Now, do you fancy another ice cream?'

And off she whizzed in her wheelchair (with a little

help from Dad). To be honest, she doesn't really need a wheelchair for anything other than long distances, but she likes queue jumping in it. She's a bit of an embarrassment at times.

I trailed slowly after her, but I didn't really fancy an ice cream. I'd made a right mess of the final and I was completely down in the dumps. Olivia and the new girl qualified for the 100 metres at the Nationals while I'd only managed to qualify for the 200 metres.

Worse still, I now knew that I could buckle under pressure. What would it be like when I was up against a real pressure expert? How would I cope if someone was determined to make me crack? To put it simply, how would I do when I raced Tom in front of the Queen on Sports Day?

11

Lili

'And what about you, Tom?'

Miss Scattergood was going round the class, finding out what topics we had all chosen for our projects. It was an increasingly frustrating experience because almost everyone had copied exactly the same phrases from exactly the same website.

'Well, Miss,' Tom said, trying to soak up as much limelight as he could with a dramatic pause, 'I thought I'd write about how rugby prepared Eric Liddell for the Olympics.'

I just about resisted the temptation to bang my head on the desk. Everything Tom says is basically about himself. He's what my Gran calls a *relentless self-promoter*.

'Oh, really, Tom?' Miss Scattergood hesitated. 'Did it? That is to say, I haven't come across rugby in anything I've read.'

'Oh yes, Miss. I've done my research, you see, and I discovered that he was a rugby player first and an athlete second. He played seven internationals and scored four tries. Guess which position he played, Miss.'

'I've really no idea, Tom,' Miss Scattergood replied, wearily lowering herself onto her chair.

'He was a winger, Miss. Just like me.'

Tariq and Andy whistled between their teeth, which I think was meant to sound some sort of approval. Miss Scattergood stood up again.

'OK, Tom, it's not quite what I had in mind but, as you say, you seem to have done your research, so that's to be commended.'

Tom grinned at her, then at me.

'And what about you, Lili?' Miss Scattergood asked, interrupting my brooding resentment. 'What topic have you chosen for your project?'

I forced myself to look at her and tried to work out what to say. I hate being late with homework. I pride myself on being organised. But this time was different.

'I couldn't make up my mind, Miss,' I said quietly.

Miss Scattergood raised an eyebrow.

'Really, Lili? That's not like you. You're usually the one I can rely on. Oh well, I suppose even the best students have their off days. Just make sure you have it sorted by next lesson, OK?'

I nodded and mumbled an apology. Miss Scattergood looked down at her markbook.

'Right, Sophie, what about you?' she continued.

I needed some time on my own when I got home but Alice was having none of it. She wanted to play. Usually I'm pretty tolerant but this time I couldn't face turning her wonky Lego castles into buildings that would stay up.

'Can we make a villerage?' she asked.

To be absolutely honest, there are times when Alice gets in the way. I love her to bits really but having a little sister is like having a super-friendly dog that just won't leave you alone.

More often than not, I wake up to find her looking down at me and when I'm walking round the house she trails round behind me, which means that one or other of us trips up whenever I change direction.

'Dad, can you look after her?' I pleaded.

'Sorry, I'm busy,' he said, turning a page of his newspaper.

I groaned. I suppose I could have gone upstairs and done my homework in the peace and quiet of my room, but I couldn't face that either, so I tried to engage Dad in conversation.

'What do you think I should do my project on?' I said, pulling his paper down so he had to look at me.

'Not another project,' he exclaimed, completely failing to answer my question. 'I thought we sent you to school to get taught. OK, OK!' He flung up his hands in mock surrender as I gave him a look. 'I won't go on but, honestly, you've got to wonder what these teachers…'

Mum caught his eye and he stopped.

'Go on, Lili,' she said. 'What are the options?'

As soon as I started to explain, Dad perked up again. I've never yet found a topic he isn't interested in, even if it's really, really obscure.

'Eric Liddell! A great guy. Yes, that'll be fun. So what were you thinking of?'

'Well, I don't know really,' I said. 'That's why I asked. I suppose I could find out more about the race he won, but…'

'But what?' Dad asked, his mind obviously elsewhere.

'But everyone else is doing that,' I continued. 'I want to do something different.'

'That's my girl!' Dad said. 'Two roads diverged in a yellow wood and all that.'

Most of the time I have no idea what he's talking about. I'm glad he never became a teacher.

'Well,' he said, throwing the newspaper onto a chair and pacing up and down the room, 'why not be a bit daring and do a project on what Eric Liddell got up to *after* the 1924 Olympics?'

I must have looked doubtful because he stopped pacing and sat down next to me. Then he got up again, grabbed an apple from the fruit bowl and bit into it.

'It's every bit as interesting as what happened at the Olympics.'

'You know what happened?' I asked.

Dad couldn't answer for a while because he'd taken far too big a bite out of the apple. He didn't set a very good example if truth be told.

'Of course I do,' he said eventually. 'Your old dad's the fount of all knowledge.'

'As long as it's of no practical use,' Mum interrupted.

'As your mother says, as long as it's of no practical use. But, on this occasion, it seems that I may have my uses. Your father's useless knowledge is going to get you through your school project. Come on, let's go into the front room. It's more comfortable there.'

I trooped after him and Alice started to troop after me until Gran stepped in and rescued me.

'Umm,' Dad said when we got there, 'we might struggle to find a seat.'

He was going through a phase of growing his own vegetables. Or trying to grow them. For some reason I didn't understand, that meant he had flower pots all over the room, including a few on the sofa and several more on the only comfy chair.

I would have thought that the best way to grow veg would be to plant them in the garden or at least to buy a greenhouse and stick them in there, but Dad had this idea that he could nurture them inside first before gradually introducing them to the wild. Reluctantly, he moved a pot off the armchair so I could sit down.

'So, what were we talking about?' he said once we'd eventually got settled.

'My project, Dad!'

'Oh yes, your project. Let's assume you choose to follow your old Dad's advice and look at the time after Eric Liddell won glory at the 1924 Olympics. What are you going to do next?'

'Well, I suppose I need to do some research,' I said.

'*Correctamente*. And where are you going to do that research?'

'On the internet, of course.'

'Ding. Wrong answer,' Dad said, whacking an imaginary bell. 'That's not how we do proper research.'

'So what do you suggest?' I asked, in what I hoped wasn't too exasperated a voice. Dad always makes things more complicated than they really need to be.

'I *suggest* that we need to look at some original documents. And if I'm not mistaken, I think we'll find that my old university has a lovely collection just waiting to be leafed through.'

I was beginning to regret asking Dad for help in the first place. Getting him involved almost always means that I end up with twice as much work as I'd started with. I tried to explain this to him, though I knew it wouldn't get me anywhere.

'Look, Dad, I'm a bit pressed for time. Surely I can find everything I need on the net?'

'Well, no you can't actually. There's a whole bunch of stuff that's not available online and, anyway, nothing beats actually going and looking. You never know what you're going to stumble across whereas—'

'But Dad...' I tried to interrupt.

He held up a hand to stop me.

'Lili, old bean, let's put it like this. If you're training for the Nationals, would you stay inside on the treadmill?'

I shook my head.

'Why not? You're still running. You're still clocking up the miles. OK, I'll tell you why not,' he continued, not giving me a chance to answer. 'Because not even the best gym can match the real thing. There's no substitute for being out on the track, feeling the firmness of the ground under your spikes, being in a real place in real weather with real people around you. It's the same with research. Not even the best website can compare with a decent library or archive. Real books. Real documents. They're the closest you're going to get to real people in the past.'

Once he gets going there's no stopping him. He was talking about a library and he looked as happy as a toddler with an Easter egg. Fortunately for me, Gran hobbled in just as he was getting into his stride. She'd been trying to read to my little sister.

'OK, that's me done with stories,' she announced. 'Next time Alice needs entertaining, I want something that's going to hold her attention for more than thirty seconds. Anyone got any ideas?'

'What do you think I should do my project on, Gran?' I asked, as much to deflect the conversation as to get an answer.

'I've no idea,' Gran replied, as Alice toddled in after her, 'but whatever your father said is probably right. He had an excellent teacher.'

'Who?' I asked. I'd never heard anything about his teachers.

Gran slumped into her armchair with a satisfied sigh.

'Me,' she said.

12

Lili

I have to give it to Tom, he took training really seriously. His technique had improved dramatically and he was now fast off the blocks. He had become a real Sports Day threat.

But I got better too.

I worked harder than ever and so my times gradually came down, though I still didn't know if it would be enough on the day.

I had the advantage of having Billy on my side though. Success isn't all in the mind. It's not just about psyching yourself up and being ruthlessly determined. The truth is that winners need other people around them. And in my case I needed Billy.

He understood me better than I understood myself. He knew when I needed pushing and when I needed a pat on the back. He knew when to talk to me and when to leave me to work it out for myself. Above all, he knew what I needed to do to improve. He was great on the details. On how to breathe properly. On how to drive with the arms and the legs. On how to stay relaxed when Harry, Mohammad or Tom were at my shoulder. Without Billy I would have had no chance.

Of course, I need my family too. I don't think about it much but I know they're always behind me. There's never any question that a competition is too far away or that training's finished too late or that it's just too cold or wet to go out again. When there's a race at the weekends we go as a family. Everyone turns out to support me: Mum, Dad, Alice and Gran too. They just get on with it so that I can get on with it.

We must look a right sight, especially now that Gran needs a wheelchair for anything apart from short distances. Plus we all look different, of course. It's not usually a problem but every now and again people do a double take when they see me and Alice with our Mum and Dad. Occasionally someone says something too, but they're usually pretty indirect. *'Is this your sister?'* or *'Are you all together?'* If anyone gets really awkward, Mum or Dad step in and deal with them while the other one takes us off for an ice cream. Looking different from your parents has its advantages sometimes.

But sometimes people can be really thoughtless when Mum and Dad aren't around and then I have to fend for myself. They ask where my 'real parents' are or make stupid comments about what I look like. I don't have to put up with too much open racism like Micah and Mohammad because people tend to be pretty positive about Chinese kids, but I do get some really stupid comments. 'You're Chinese: you must be good at maths.' That sort of thing. It's really annoying because I am quite good at maths but I wasn't always good at it. I've had to work really hard. It's nothing to do with my race or my genes: it's just that I got my head down and stuck at it. But not everyone appreciates that. They think it just comes naturally.

Maybe that's why I took up athletics. Nobody expects to see a Chinese sprinter (even though there have been some really good ones). So if I do all right in a race they're less likely to think it's because of my race, if you see what I mean.

Actually, I quite like that: *it's not all about the race.* Maybe I'll use it as the title of my project.

But sometimes it just gets too much and then I don't want to hang aroud and justify why I am who I am. When it's like that I head back home, shut myself in my bedroom and get my adoption photos out of the cupboard. There's one of me looking bewildered as we pose for our first family portrait and another of me in some sort of government building where the adoption took place. I'm wearing a little red dress and my foot is covered in red ink. I know, it's all a bit odd, but because I was too young to sign my name they had to take a footprint instead.

I've got other photos in my adoption album too,

earlier ones. Ones they took when I was in foster care. I'm not sure what to think about them. I always look padded up in clothes that are too big for me and I'm a bit grubby. I can't help wondering what sort of house it was where I spent that first year and a half of my life. I haven't got a photo of the building itself, but from what I can see of the background it must have been a bit run down. There's not much furniture and there's no sign of any toys, apart from a blue plastic baby stroller which I'm propped up in.

There isn't any sign of anyone else either, but I know there were other people in the house. The man and woman who looked after me, for a start, and their birth children (though I don't know how many of them there were). And some other children who were being fostered like me. There was a girl who was adopted by a family in the USA about the same time Mum and Dad adopted me, and another girl who was adopted by a family in Spain. I guess I must have spent a lot of time with them when I was a baby but I can't remember anything about them now. I sometimes wonder if they became athletes too.

I don't often reach back beyond that. But sometimes in quiet moments I think about my birth parents. I don't know anything about them but, in my imagination, I see them as a prince and princess. I know that isn't really possible because China doesn't have a king and queen. In

THE RACE

fact, it doesn't even have an emperor any more because they got rid of their last one over a hundred years ago. My mum and dad say that my birth parents loved me and wanted the very best for me, but that circumstances can sometimes be very difficult. They might have been very poor or maybe they came under huge pressure from their community or the government. It's impossible to tell, but that doesn't stop me wondering what they looked like and what they were like as people.

Sometimes people say this all happened when I was so young that it didn't affect me. I guess they're trying to be helpful but they really aren't. My mum's a really level-headed person but that sort of comment is pretty much the only thing that annoys her. She takes a deep breath and then calmly goes through all the reasons why it *does* matter. That usually shuts them up.

Then she gives me a hug and sometimes we have a chat and sometimes we don't. If we do, she tells me that when I was really little I had to fend for myself. I had to make myself heard and I had to get myself noticed, otherwise I wouldn't have got the attention I needed. Or even the food and drink I needed. I had to be competitive to survive. That's probably why I'm so fiercely determined today.

But sometimes I get sad when Mum and Dad are doing the washing or preparing a meal and I don't really know why. We've talked about that too. Mum tells me that it might be because I didn't get all the cuddles and kisses I needed when I was a little baby. It sounds funny but I know she's right, partly because she's my mum and partly because she studied all this stuff at university. 'What babies need is love,' she says. 'And not just babies.' Then she gives me another hug and I feel much better.

13

Eric
Paris, July 1924

Eric was back in the Colombes Stadium but this time not for a rugby match. He was there for the Olympics, competing against the world's greatest athletes in the world's greatest sporting event. He was still a university student but he had qualified for the final of the 400 metres.

As he walked onto the track, he looked around and took a deep breath as he remembered playing rugby there for Scotland. He remembered that knot of excitement as the anthems played, the intensity of the first half, and the torrential downpour that threatened to wash out the rest of the match. He had played several more matches since then and the conditions had never been as bad. And now he was back in perfect sprinting weather. It was going to be a great day.

Taking one last look round, he said a prayer. A prayer of thanks, not a prayer for victory. He knew that there was no guarantee of success because God was not a hand on his back or a stronger pair of legs.

'It's time to warm up, Liddell. You're on next,' a voice called out. It was Joe Binks, the journalist and former world record holder. 'And if you want my advice, you'll run like mad and let the others catch you.'

Eric gave a grateful nod of thanks because Binks had confirmed what he already planned to do: go flat out from the start as if he was running the 100 metres and then try to hang on.

It wouldn't be easy because the competition was stiff. Josef Imbach from Switzerland had set a new Olympic record in the quarter-finals, only for that record to be broken in the semi-finals by the USA's Horatio Fitch. Eric's team-mate Guy Butler, who had already won a Gold and a Silver at the 1920 Olympics, would also be a medal contender. If Eric was going to have any chance of winning this race for which he had not properly trained, he would have to run the race of his life.

He'd been drawn in the outside lane, which was usually regarded as the trickiest lane of all, but he decided that it was, in fact, an advantage. He could concentrate on his own race while the others watched him fly away from the start. If he could put them under pressure then maybe, just maybe, he would be in with a chance.

The starter called them to their marks. The roar of the crowd grew louder. Eric checked his foot holes, stretched each leg in turn, and then placed his fingers carefully behind the line. When he was ready, he looked up at the track in front of him. It was the first ten metres that mattered. If he could surge away from the start, if he could hit his stride quickly, there was no one in the world who could catch him. Not over 100 metres anyway. Then it would be a case of digging deeper than he had ever dug before. For most of the race he would be hanging on.

As the crowd became silent, he reached deep inside himself to a place that no one other than God could enter. He breathed in and waited for the gun to fire. All his hard work over the last two years had been leading up to this point.

The crowd disappeared. The other runners became a blur. It was just Eric and the starting gun.

And then he was away. Running flat out and accelerating into the first bend. Arms pumping, legs striding out, breath pulsing. He was doing what he did best. Running. Running fast. Running free.

14

Lili

'OK, I've booked us into the archives,' Dad announced.

I'd forgotten all about his crazy plan, to be honest, but he most definitely hadn't.

'Yep, I got on the old internet and found a slot. Next Tuesday at 11am, you and I are going to find out everything there is to know about Eric Liddell.'

I thought it was a bit ironic that he'd used the internet to book us in, given all that stuff about doing research in real books, but I let it pass, mainly because I had to break it to him gently that I was supposed to be at school on Tuesdays.

'No sweat,' Dad said. 'I'll just write to Mrs Whatshername or Mr... You know, the one who's in charge. It's an educational visit. It won't be a problem.'

But of course it was a problem, just like I knew it would be.

'I'm sorry, Mr DeLisle, there are strict rules about this sort of thing,' Mrs Hughes explained, when Dad came into school for a meeting. 'Visiting a university at Lili's age doesn't really fit any of our categories.'

'But she's doing historical research! She's going to be learning stuff, which the last time I checked is what schools are supposed to be interested in,' Dad replied.

I thought he was going to make a comment about project work too, but somehow he resisted the temptation. I squirmed with embarrassment in my seat.

'I know, I know,' Mrs Hughes replied. 'It's very commendable that you're taking an interest in your daughter's education but—'

'I'm not taking an interest,' Dad interrupted. 'I'm her father. I'm the primary educator and you're *in loco parentis*. I have temporarily allowed you to educate my daughter while I get on with earning a living. However, next Tuesday I'm resuming my teaching responsibilities and will be taking Lili to the university archives. As a matter of courtesy I have let you know. I'm not asking permission.'

'Well, I'm afraid it will have to go down as an unauthorised absence,' Mrs Hughes said rather frostily.

'Fine. Go for it,' my dad replied. 'School refuses permission for daughter to learn stuff. No wonder this country's in a mess.'

'Sorry, Mrs Hughes,' I whispered as we left. 'He gets carried away sometimes.'

'Don't worry, sweetie,' she whispered back. 'I can see he's passionate about your education. I won't take it personally.'

It had gone pretty much as badly as it could have done and I just wanted out. But getting out of the office didn't get us out of the school. We still had a long walk down the corridor of shame. There were hundreds of people about and, unfortunately for me, one of them was Tom.

'Oi, Lili, in trouble again?' he called out in a voice that couldn't be ignored.

I stopped in my tracks, set my face to pleasant and turned to face him.

'Tom, how lovely to see you. No, not in trouble, just having a chat with Mrs Hughes.'

Tom barked a dismissive laugh.

'Right,' he said. 'And who's this with you?'

He knew full well who Dad was because he'd seen him at a whole bunch of school events. He was just being unpleasant. Again.

'This is my dad,' I replied politely.

Tom pulled a face.

'Really?' he said. 'I wouldn't have thought...'

But he didn't get to finish whatever nastiness it was he was going to say because Dad interrupted him.

'So you must be the famous Tom,' he said. 'I've heard all about you.'

He peered at him like he was an exhibit in a museum, which threw Tom completely. He stepped back and pulled another face.

'That's right,' he said. 'I'm Tom. The famous Tom. The

infamous Tom.'

Adam Carter, who was hovering at his elbow, sniggered loudly, though I'm pretty sure he had no idea what *infamous* meant.

'I wouldn't be so sure about the "infamous" part, Dad said. 'You have to be really bad to be infamous and, from what I hear tell, you're just irritating. But it was nice to meet you anyway.'

And without waiting for any further comment, he was off. I stayed for a moment to give Tom my broadest smile and then trotted after him.

'You can't say that to people, Dad,' I whispered as we walked out the front door.

'*Au contraire*, my lovely,' he replied. 'I just did.'

I quite enjoyed Dad's put down but I still wasn't very happy about the meeting with Mrs Hughes, so I tried staying quiet to express my disapproval. Dad didn't notice. The problem is that he quite enjoys winding teachers up. He sees it as a sort of public service. I'll never forget the day he stood up at prizegiving and pointed out that they'd put an apostrophe in the wrong place in the programme. I would have run out and hid if I hadn't been stuck in the middle of a row.

'Well, I thought that went quite well, didn't you, Lili?' he said as we pulled up at some red lights.

'No, Dad, I really didn't. It was horribly, horribly embarrassing.'

'Ah yes, that most teenagery of words: embarrassing,' he replied. 'A shame so few of you can spell it.'

I groaned and tried to pretend this conversation wasn't happening.

'Yes, we're going to have a great time at uni,' he continued. 'There's nothing like getting your hands on real documents. Films are great. They grab your emotions and give them a good old shake but sometimes they make a mess of what actually happened. I mean, *Chariots of Fire* is a wonderful movie but it gets some pretty important facts wrong, wouldn't you agree?'

'I don't know, Dad,' I said. 'I've never seen it.'

'Never seen it? Really? Well I never. How did that happen?'

He looked genuinely bemused.

'Maybe because you never showed it to me,' I suggested.

'Well, there's only one way to fix that,' he continued. 'We'll just have to watch it this weekend.'

'Sounds good to me,' I said.

And it was. After dinner on Saturday, Alice and I got into our pyjamas and dressing gowns while Gran settled down for a read, Mum prepared popcorn, and Dad tried to find the DVD.

'I know it's here somewhere,' he muttered. 'I saw it the other day.'

Once he'd eventually tracked it down in the *Sound*

of Music box set, we all snuggled up on the sofa and pressed play.

The first thing that struck me was how old it all seemed. The title sequence looked really amateurish and the colour was a bit faded. But the next thing that hit me was the music. It was really stirring stuff. It surged out of the screen while the athletes ran along a beach and it made me all emotional. And that was even before the film had really got going.

'They filmed that at St Andrew's,' Dad said because he loves giving a running commentary whenever we're watching a movie. 'I used to play golf there.'

'Really?' Mum said, looking sceptical.

'Yep, on the beach. I couldn't afford the actual golf course, but I can say I've played out of the sand at St Andrew's.'

'Shh, Daddy, I'm trying to watch,' Alice interrupted. And to my surprise, he did.

I won't go through the movie scene by scene but I have to mention two things that really stood out. The first was the way Eric Liddell ran. He was all over the place. His head was flung back and his arms were flailing around. Billy would never have let him get away with running like that. But the other really striking thing was his quiet assurance. He didn't have any of the cockiness of the athletes you see at the Olympics today. He just got on with it calmly. And by 'it', I mean winning the 400 metres, even though he hadn't really trained for it.

'Except he had, of course,' Dad said. 'He found out months before the Olympics that the 100 metre heats were going to be held on a Sunday, so he had a decent amount of time to adjust.'

'So the film got it all wrong?' I said, while Mum carried Alice up to bed. She'd fallen asleep almost as soon as the film started.

'Not all wrong,' Dad said. 'He really was better at the 100 and 200 metres and so no one expected that he would win the 400. He was a quite remarkable athlete.'

'And did he really run like that, with his head back and his arms rolling?'

'Well, I'm not sure. I think he was a bit unorthodox, though I don't know if it was quite as bad as they suggest in the film. Maybe that's something you can find out about for your project. That and what happened next, after the Olympics. That's what's missing from the movie. And that, Lili, is the really interesting bit.'

15

Lili

The next day I tried to find some footage of the 1924 Olympics on YouTube. To be honest, I was a bit hazy about when they invented video but I searched anyway and, to my surprise, I found some. Two minutes of really grainy film, showing an unidentified sprint race and then the final of the 400 metres.

The camera angles were terrible. Eric disappeared out of shot almost immediately and then, when the director cut to the final straight, it was difficult to see just how close any of the runners were. Even so, it was still pretty dramatic. There were ropes tied onto little poles between each of the lanes and one of the runners tripped over his just metres from the end and never finished. But the result was never in doubt. Eric Liddell fired out of the start and stayed out in front till the very end.

The other thing that came across really clearly was the cinder track they used. It must have been like running on firm sand but, even so, they were all really quick. But no one was quicker than Eric Liddell. He really bombed down the track. I kept on replaying the video until it was firmly stuck in my head. The surge from the start, the head going back as he rounded the final bend, the applause of the crowd. A guy smoking a pipe came over to congratulate him at the end and he hardly looked out of breath. Eric Liddell, that is. Not the guy with the pipe.

Once I'd watched that film, Eric wasn't a character in a history book any more. He was real. An athlete like me. For the first time I actually felt quite pleased that Dad was taking me out of school so I could find out more about him.

Quite pleased but not pleased enough to stop worrying about skiving a day of school. That's why, when Tuesday came, I tried to persuade Dad to phone in and say that I was ill. It wouldn't look so bad that way. He refused point blank.

'What are you talking about, Lili? You're not ill, are you? And surely you're not suggesting that I should lie to your Mrs Whatsisname?'

'I'm not suggesting you lie, just that you help me out of a difficult situation.'

'Oh come on, Lili, you're not really worried about that Mrs… What is she called again?'

'Mrs Hughes, Dad! No, I'm not worried, I'd just rather not have the embarrassment of ignoring what she told us not to do, if that makes sense. It's called saving face. We learned about it at school.'

'Well, I'm glad you've learned something in that

place. I was beginning to wonder. Anyway, we'd better get going or we're going to miss the train.'

Suddenly Dad sprang into action and I had little choice but to rush after him. Clearly the phone call wasn't going to happen.

We raced to the car and then he really put his foot down, which isn't great news because he's not the safest driver at the best of times. We hurtled through the streets and somehow we got to the station without crashing, though the stress of the journey completely took it out of me. Collapsing into a seat on the train, I closed my eyes and tried to catch my breath.

As we trundled through the countryside I slowly began to relax. It hadn't been a great start to the day but I figured I might as well enjoy not being in school now the decision had been taken out of my hands. The only problem was that Dad relaxed too. And when he relaxes he talks a lot, which can be pretty awkward when there are other people around. Fortunately the carriage was virtually empty so I let him talk away while I unpacked the enormous packed lunch that Mum had made for us. It was only half nine in the morning but Dad didn't seem to mind.

'Dad,' I interrupted after he'd burbled on for a bit, 'why didn't Eric Liddell run on a Sunday? I mean, I know he was religious but I still don't get why running on a Sunday is a problem.'

'Good question, little one,' Dad replied, leaning back in his seat and taking an enormous bite out of his cheese sandwich. 'Let's put it like this: we all pay attention to what really matters to us and what mattered to Liddell was God. Sunday, as far as he was concerned, was a day off from the usual nonsense. A day off from emails and mobile phones. That's me rather than Liddell, of course: he was lucky enough to live in an age when phones were tied to the wall like dangerous dogs.'

I let him ramble on because he was obviously enjoying himself. Meanwhile I tried to work out what he was talking about.

'So let me get this straight, Dad,' I said after he'd gone on for a few more minutes. 'You're saying he didn't run on Sundays because he wanted to concentrate?'

'Not concentrate, little one: pay attention. It's a different thing. We concentrate on problems: we pay attention to people.'

'But God's not a person,' I said.

'That's precisely who he is,' Dad said, spraying crumbs across the carriage in his indignation. 'They clearly don't teach you about the Council of Chalcedon at school. One God in three persons. Which means, among other things, that you need to give him time, especially on Sundays.'

I looked out of the window to help me get my thoughts in order.

'So, does that mean I shouldn't be running on Sundays either?' I asked

Dad put down the Cherry Bakewell he'd just picked up and looked at me intensely. 'What do you think?' he said.

'I don't know. That's why I'm asking.'

'I think you do know,' he said. 'I think you know how to pay attention to what really matters. You know what's important and what's not. That's why you didn't want to skip school today.

'But—'

Dad interrupted me.

'I'm not just talking about school,' he said. 'I'm talking about important stuff. Let me put it like this: when your mother and I realised that you have a real athletics talent, we made a decision. We decided we'd support you in any way we could, but we also decided that we'd do it together. When you have an athletics meet, we go as a family. When you're powering down the back straight, we're all right behind you. But we weren't going to squeeze God out to support you. So we also decided that we'd still get to Church every Sunday, no matter where you're competing.'

'So does that mean Eric Liddell was wrong?'

'No, it doesn't mean he was wrong. It just means he had a different way of paying attention to what matters. Does that make sense? I hope so because this Cherry

Bakewell is sitting up and begging to be eaten.'

I nodded, he grinned, and the Cherry Bakewell disappeared whole.

16

Lili

The university archive was a strange old place. We had to lock our bags away in a locker like the ones you get at swimming pools, for a start, and we were only allowed to take pencils in with us.

'There's nothing allowed in here that could ruin the documents,' the lady at the desk explained. 'No pens, no water... and no children either usually, but today we've made an exception as your father's well known to us.'

I didn't ask her what she meant by that. I didn't really want to know.

Dad had ordered some documents in advance so there were three boxes all ready for us on the table, the first of which was filled with stuff that once belonged to Eric Liddell: letters, photographs, reports, drawings and a whole lot more besides.

I pulled out one of the letters and settled down for a good read. I have to admit that it was amazing. The paper was so thin I was surprised it had survived all these years and the handwriting was really neat. Eric must have been a very careful writer. I found a book he'd written as well. He'd typed it all out but had added immaculately written comments in the margin. Seeing his handwriting on a book that was almost 100 years old felt really odd. It was like he was still alive, working in an office in some distant part of China while I was sitting in the archive.

I leafed through the box to see what else I could find and picked out a flyer for a talk: *Eric Liddell (Rugby International—Olympic Champion Runner—Missionary to China) will speak in YMCA, Wednesday 27th April, 3.30pm, the High Sheriff, Councillor F.J. Holland, in the chair.*

It was a bit irritating that they'd put rugby international before Olympic champion, but it was the missionary to China bit that really caught my eye.

'That's what he did after the Olympics,' Dad said with a smile. 'No hanging around celebrities or appearing on daytime TV for our Eric. He finished his degree, jumped on a train to China and took up a teaching job in a place called Tientsin.'

'He became a teacher?' I said. 'That doesn't sound very heroic.'

'Depends what sort of school you're teaching in,' Dad replied. 'But you're right. Being a teacher was too comfortable for our Eric so he waited until the Japanese invaded and then set off for a war-torn part of the country called Siaochang, where his brother Rob was working as a doctor. I'm not sure what his wife made of it.'

'He was married?'

It came about a bit loud. In fact, it probably came out really loud because even Dad looked over his shoulder to check whether the librarian was going to have a go at us.

'You might want to keep your voice down in here, little one,' he suggested. 'They have slightly old-fashioned notions about not disturbing other people while they're working. But, in answer to your question, yes he was married. To Florence, another missionary. And, before you ask, they had three children, Patricia, Heather and Maureen, though Eric never saw Maureen.'

'Why ever not?'

'Because the war got in the way of normal family life, that's why. Eric knew how much danger his family would be in if they stayed in China so he sent his two children and his pregnant wife away to safety in Canada. And then... well, he wasn't able to rejoin them, let's put it like that.'

I gulped. That didn't sound too good. In fact, it sounded really bad.

'When you say 'danger', what exactly do you mean?' I whispered because the librarian was now definitely glaring in our direction.

'I mean the invading forces were pretty ruthless and the Chinese warlords weren't always much better. It was pretty chaotic at that time in parts of China. Law and order had broken down and there were groups of armed men wandering around, robbing and looting whatever they could get their hands on. There's a document in here somewhere about Eric and his brother following in the footsteps of the retreating Chinese army. It was 1937 and—''

'Wait a minute,' I whispered.

I was confused.

'World War II started in 1939, so why was the Chinese army retreating in 1937?'

Dad shook his head.

'They really don't teach you much at that school of yours, do they?' he said ruefully. 'Yes, World War II started in 1939 but not for the Chinese. The Japanese had already taken some of their land in 1931 and then in 1937 they invaded to make double sure that it stayed in Japanese hands. The Chinese army was a bit of a mess at the time so it was swept away. That's why Eric Liddell had such a tricky time getting about. Sometimes he had to negotiate with a local warlord and sometimes with the Japanese.'

'And did it work?' I whispered behind my hand because I could see the librarian glaring in our direction again.

'Well, sort of,' Dad whispered back.

'What do you mean 'sort of'?' I asked, but this time the librarian had had enough. She came over to our desk, put her hands on her hips and gave us a dressing down.

'I'm sorry,' she said, though to be honest she didn't look sorry at all, 'but I'm going to have to warn you that any more talking in here and I'm going to have to take further measures.'

Dad smiled at her.

'You mean you're going to throw us out?'

The librarian hrumphed and walked back to her desk.

'I suspect that means "yes",' Dad whispered. 'We'd better do as we're told.'

It was all a bit awkward. Some of the other researchers were staring at us as well so, as much to give myself something to do as anything else, I put my hand in the cardboard box and pulled out another piece of paper. To my surprise, it wasn't another letter but a painting of a flower. A peony, the caption said. It was painted in the Chinese style with clear brush strokes and just a few basic colours. It was very beautiful.

'I wonder why he kept a picture of a flower?' I said, before clapping my hand over my mouth. I pulled a face at Dad and refused to look in the direction of the librarian.

Dad grinned, looked over his shoulder to check the coast was clear, and then whispered a quick explanation that didn't explain very much at all.

'It was a gift,' he said. 'Here, have a look at this. It'll explain things better than I can.'

17

Eric
Siaochang, China 1937

Our journey to Siaochang was extremely difficult. Railway lines had been blown up, villages had been destroyed, and many of the roads were impassable, so we travelled mostly by river. That was no easier. We were robbed three times and arrived in such an exhausted state that we were immediately admitted to the hospital as patients ourselves!

However, we soon recovered and set to work, for the need was very great. One evening, for instance, I was given a garbled message about a badly wounded man who had been abandoned in one of the Buddhist temples. No one dared treat him for fear of the Japanese, so his life hung in the balance. Without proper medical treatment he would undoubtedly die.

I sent my carter to the area and, a short time afterwards, followed him on my bicycle, stopping only to gain support from the local Headman (for we can do little in these parts without them). From him I discovered that a Japanese tank and ten motor lorries were stationed in the very next village, a mere mile away, which meant that we had to work quickly and carefully. I hurried onto the temple and was appalled by what I found.

The wounded man was in a terrible state. He was covered with nothing more than an old flea-infested blanket, and his wounds were seeping with pus. I did what I could but I knew that if I did not get him to our hospital at Siaochang he would soon die. With the help of my carter, I placed him on our cart ready for the eighteen-mile journey.

But that was not the end of our troubles. While rushing back by a roundabout route to avoid the Japanese, we were intercepted by some Chinese villagers who told us about another victim of this appalling war. Six Chinese soldiers had been rounded up and sentenced to death by beheading. Five of them were killed, but the sixth had refused to kneel down as commanded, which prompted a furious swing of the sword from his guard. Somehow the poor man survived. When the villagers emerged from their houses, they found him, unconscious but still breathing. They carried him to a temple, where he too now lay at death's door.

Desperate as we were to return to Siaochang, we could not abandon the poor fellow, so we made the detour and found him propped up in a dark and dirty corner with his cloak wrapped around his neck as a bandage.

Scarcely believing that he would survive the journey, we placed him on the cart next to the other patient and hurried back the way we had come.

By God's providence, we arrived safely at our destination without further incident and so were able to entrust our patients to the care of our doctors. Then we waited and prayed. After a few days, the first man was called to his eternal rest but, to our amazement, the second survived.

Over the next few weeks the two of us became good friends and spent many happy hours together while he slowly recuperated. His name was Li Tsin Sheng and he was a fine amateur artist, his recovery no doubt being hastened by the work he did with his brush.

One day he seemed peculiarly caught up in a painting, but when I asked him the nature of his work he refused to answer. I soon discovered why. He was painting a picture of a peony flower, a symbol of beauty emerging from the dirt. I thought it very beautiful and I was greatly touched when he gave it to me as a token of thanks.

It is years since I last saw him and, since that time, I have lost almost everything I once owned. But, through all the disasters of these years, I have held onto that picture. It is nailed to the wall above my bed now. Every morning it lifts my spirits. Every evening it reminds me that hands of friendship still stretch out across the oceans. In that one simple picture Scotland and China are united.

18

Lili

Billy wasn't very happy with me. It was the first time I'd seen him since the Regional Championships and he was really miffed.

'I could understand it if you were beaten by a better runner,' he said, 'but it sounds to me as if you just got complacent.'

I hung my head in shame.

'Don't stand there with that hangdog expression,' he continued. 'The way to deal with complacency is to train. Train the body and train the mind. If you're going to compete nationally you need to be ready for anything.'

I tried to look ready.

'And if you're going to win Sports Day you need to be ready for anything plus Tom.'

I grinned.

'OK, Billy, message received and understood. I'm going to sort myself out.'

'Good girl,' he said, smiling. 'So let's get running.'

We trained really hard that session. Really really hard given how hot it was. Unusually for Billy in mid-season, we focused on strength work. We did sit-ups and press-ups, followed by circuits and yet more sit-ups. Just when I thought he was going to take pity on us, he launched into a whole load more. It was exhausting.

And then Tom showed up.

'Just look at these beauties!' he announced, holding a pair of running shoes up to his ears as though they were bulbous earrings.

'Is that, *"I'm really sorry I'm late, Billy. It won't happen again."*?' Billy asked with more than a touch of sarcasm in his voice.

'No, it's just look at these beauties,' Tom replied. He was never much good at picking up on subtleties. 'Mum texted me to say they'd arrived so I had to get back home before training. There's no way I'm running without them.'

It's true that they were a nice pair of spikes. You could tell just by looking at them that they were really expensive too. Not that that bothered me. Expensive things are usually expensive to appeal to the vanity of the fools who buy them. That's what my Gran taught me and I reckon she's pretty much right.

What really bothered me was the realisation that Tom was preparing so carefully for the race. I'd half thought he was going to run it in rugby boots, but if he'd gone to the trouble of buying a proper set of running spikes then he must be really serious. Not that he would have paid for them himself, of course.

I've got to give it to Billy, though. Nothing phases him and he's always one step ahead of the opposition. Rather than get into a slanging match with Tom about being on time, he simply adapted his training session.

'Right then, troops,' he announced. 'Time for some 800 metre circuits.'

Everyone groaned, apart from Tom who complained.

'You've got to be joking!' he said. 'These are sprinting spikes. I can't run the 800 in them!'

'Then you ought to come better prepared,' Billy told him. 'Now get in line. We've got work to do.'

And work we did. He made us do circuit after circuit until half of us went down with cramp and Tom became almost tearful with anger.

'I hate this poxy training camp,' he muttered.

'Then maybe you should try out an easier sport,' Billy said. 'Something like rugby, for instance.'

I covered a grin with my hand and Tom stormed off. It was a pretty good way to end the session.

———

Gran let me in when I got home because Mum had popped out to the shops and Dad wasn't back from work.

'Just you and me,' she announced gleefully, 'which means you can forget all about homework and have a good old chinwag instead.'

Forgetting about homework sounded good to me and talking to Gran was always entertaining. Besides which, I knew that Mum wouldn't be at the shops forever, so I might as well enjoy my freedom while it lasted. Slinging my bag onto the floor and myself onto a beanbag, I gave Gran a big, beaming smile.

'You're on,' I said.

Gran beamed back. The look on her face never ceased to warm me through.

'Where's Alice?' I asked as we snuggled down.

'She's in her room building a castle or a beauty parlour or something,' Gran replied. 'Something to do with Lego anyway.'

To be honest, Gran's never really taken childcare seriously. I can sometimes persuade her to step in and play Jenga or Dobble with Alice when she's getting under my feet, but it's always a risk. Either she forgets what she's supposed to be doing and wanders off halfway through a game, or the two of them have so much fun together that I want to join in myself, which destroys the whole point of the exercise.

'She's very quiet,' I said.

Gran thumped herself on the forehead.

'Oh yes, that's because she's not there at all. I forgot. Your mum took her shopping. I offered to babysit but she said I wasn't to be trusted.' She smiled cheerfully. 'She's probably right.'

I rolled my eyes. Some people say that you gain wisdom with age. Gran simply becomes more irresponsible.

'So how are you getting on with your campaign to out-nice Tom?' she asked.

It was a good question. The truth of the matter was that it was going pretty well. Every time I saw Tom I felt a sharp stab of irritation, which I covered up with a broad smile. After a while I had discovered to my surprise that I actually felt different.

'Do you know what, Gran?' I replied. 'I feel sorry for him now. It must be hard work having to be that objectionable all the time.'

'Great,' Gran said. 'Before you know it, you'll end up liking him.'

'Fat chance!' I said, pulling a face.

Gran wrinkled her nose in mock disgust.

'And how did you get on with your day trip to the library?' she said.

'Oh, pretty well,' I replied breezily.

'I believe that's what's called a non-answer,' Gran said. 'So let me try again. What did you learn on your day off school?'

I grinned.

'OK, sorry Gran. I found out all about what Eric Liddell got up to after the 1924 Olympics. Well, actually not all about it. There are still a few details I need to clear up.'

Gran started picking her nose. There was nothing she enjoyed more than not acting her age. She really was quite extraordinary. Her favourite badge was one which read 'Growing old gracefully. Not!' She wore it whenever she could get away with it, which meant that going out with her could be pretty embarrassing. When she wasn't showing shop assistants her badge, she was wolf whistling builders or playing with her yoyo in the queue at the bank. On one memorable Saturday evening she even tried to climb over a wall into the local park and was caught by a policeman. 'I wanted to find out if I could still do it,' she told him. She was 83 years old at the time and her legs were a lot stronger then.

'Ah, that's better,' she said. 'So what exactly do you need to find out?'

'Well,' I said, drawing my knees up to my chin, 'I know that Eric won gold in the 400 metres at the Olympics and I know that he went back to China afterwards. Then there was a war with Japan which kind of merged into World War II.'

'And...'

'And he saved two Chinese soldiers who were being hunted down by the Japanese, except one of them died and then... well, I'm not sure what happened next. The documents in the archive don't say what happened after 1941. I could google it of course but Dad's right: seeing letters that Eric Liddell wrote himself has changed things. I want a bit more than a webpage.'

'And…'

'And then—' I continued.

'No!' Gran said, interrupting my interruption. 'When I said "and" it wasn't a prompt for you to keep going. It was me trying to get a word in edgeways.'

I grinned again and apologised, though to be perfectly honest it's sometimes safest not to let Gran get a word in edgeways.

'And,' she said, briefly closing her eyes as though preparing to meditate, 'the trail goes cold in 1941? That's a rhetorical question: there's no need for you to say anything. But we know that he died in China at some point. Do you know when?'

'Nope,' I said, 'but I don't mind googling something as simple as that.'

Which I did, while Gran sadly shook her head.

'1945,' I said.

'Aged 43 or thereabouts,' Gran added. 'Not such good news. Well, we know what happened in 1945: the war ended and Eric Liddell died. What we don't know is what happened between 1941 and 1945. That is, *you* don't know.'

I sat up in surprise, though I suppose nothing about Gran should have surprised me, least of all her incredible general knowledge.

'Are you saying that *you* know?' I asked.

'Well, I know what happened in 1941, having lived through it myself, which means that I have a pretty shrewd suspicion about what must have happened to your Eric.'

Then she closed both eyes and gave every indication that she was about to settle down for a little sleep. I wasn't letting her get away with that, so I manoeuvred myself off the bean bag and snuggled up next to her.

'Come on, Gran!' I said. 'You can't leave it there. What happened in 1941?'

She flicked one eye open, like a wary meerkat.

'I can't tell you everything, Lili dear. There are some things you are just going to have to find out for yourself.'

I groaned deeply.

'You sound just like Dad,' I complained.

'I know,' she said. 'He got all his worst habits from me.'

Then she flicked off her shoes, closed her eyes again and stretched herself out on the sofa with a very satisfied sigh.

19

Eric
Tientsin, China, 1941

As the fighting grew worse, we were forced to make a decision, the most difficult decision we had yet faced during the long years of conflict. Should we stay in Siaochang with our suffering people or evacuate to Tientsin? Rob and I were all for staying, even though we knew that our position was growing daily more precarious. The hospital had been attacked and looted by both sides. Most of our equipment and all of our medicine had been stolen. Our food supplies were at a critically low level and even our well was running dry. Our hospital was a hospital only in name.

We gave little thought for our own safety but when some of our patients fell into a terrible decline, we knew that we had no choice but to leave. They would not survive if we did not get them better care. Most of our congregation chose to stay in their village but we managed to persuade all our patients to travel with us, even though we knew that it would be a perilous journey.

We left at dawn with little more than the clothes on our backs. Those who could walk walked. Those who could not were pushed on our few basic carts. We got as far as the river without incident but, as we waited for a boat we feared might never arrive, we lost our last remaining valuables. A Japanese patrol took a fancy to our jackets and Rob's watch, which he had somehow kept all this time. I thought of Florence and the children back in Tientsin and, thanking God that he had kept them safe, resolved to send them abroad at the earliest opportunity. In Canada they would be safe: in China every day was uncertain.

Eventually a boat came. After torturous negotiations we managed to persuade the captain to take our party upriver. (Of course, he was no captain but a ruffian who had found or stolen the vessel.) We gave him what little money we had and promised him more if he could deliver us to our families. He pushed us for as much as he could get, but it was clear that underneath his show of bravado he was terrified. Trusting no one, he feared everyone, his passengers as much as the soldiers he thought we would meet around every bend of the river.

We did meet them too. Some of them ignored us, some taunted us, and a few roughed us up when they discovered that we were poorer than they. On more than one occasion our captain refused to sail any further until we bullied him into courage. The poor man was wholly unfit for the task. He had been born into an era of conflict but had a heart that was fitted only for peace.

It was a terrible journey but, after many troubles, we finally reached Tientsin, where we were met by our friends. They had heard that a party of 'white ghosts', as we are sometimes called in these parts, were sailing downriver and had rushed out to see whether the rumour was true. They were delighted to welcome us back to Tientsin but could not keep expressions of shock from their faces. When we looked at ourselves in a mirror for the first time in many days, we understood why. Our beards were long, our faces dirty, and bones stuck out from our emaciated bodies. We had not eaten properly for weeks and what little we had we had shared with our unfortunate patients.

By the grace of God, the patients had all survived, though we did not know whether they would ever fully recover, even with such care as we were now able to offer them in Tientsin. However, we had done our duty and so were able to leave them at the hospital and hurry back to our families, hoping that the war would not pursue us. It proved to be a forlorn hope.

Shortly after we arrived in Tientsin we heard news of the Japanese attack on Pearl Harbour. Then the USA and Great Britain declared war on Japan. We were now the enemy.

20

Lili

I was chatting to Sophie in the playground when Tom came sauntering over to see us.

'How's your project going, Lilian?' he asked with a sneer in his voice. 'Found out any more about that famous rugby player yet?'

Resisting the temptation to rugby tackle him myself, I smiled instead and served up a juicy fact I had discovered in the library. I'd been biding my time to sock this one to him.

'It's going pretty well, actually. Everything I've read so far has confirmed that he really was Chinese. And British too, of course.'

'Oh yeah?' Tom said.

'Yeah. Do you know what his name was?

'Eric!' Tom said, rolling his eyes like I'd gone completely potty.

'*Li Airu*,' I corrected him. 'That was his Chinese name. And before you ask, the surname comes first in China. *Li* as in Liddell and *Airu* as in Eric.'

For a moment he looked uncertain, but then he turned

his back on me with an arrogant 'As if' and wandered away. Victory to me, I thought, if only in the first heat.

Tom must have thought so too because he did everything he could to batter me into submission at our next training session. There were only four weeks until Sports Day now and he knew as well as I did that the battle between us was going to be as much in our minds as in our bodies. Neither of us was going to get much quicker in a month, but we could certainly have a good go at psyching each other out. Tom clearly thought he had an advantage in that area, being a boy, whereas I reckoned I had an advantage, being cunning. He was about as cunning as a sledgehammer.

Every time we had a training session Tom positioned himself next to me. He was there when we worked on our starts, when we accelerated over thirty metres, and even when we were jogging round the track. He obviously thought he was going to wear me down with his manly presence.

I decided to ignore him and concentrate on what Billy was saying instead, especially since I knew that Billy was on my side. Everything we did at training was for my benefit and not for Tom's. Even so, it was difficult to blank him out completely. He made so much noise for a start. If he wasn't grunting he was muttering insults. And if he wasn't muttering insults he was urging himself on. It was like training in front of a TV you can't turn down.

But even his ridiculous noises didn't bother me too much because I knew that I was running well. Really well. Despite the disaster at the Regionals, I was on top form. I was quick out of the blocks. My pick up was great and my running style was relaxed and efficient. I was as quick as I'd ever been and Tom must have known it.

Billy must have known it too because he did what he rarely did, which was actually allow us to race. We had a 60 metre sprint near the start of the session, which I won. Then an 80 metres race at the end of the session. I won that too, but only just. I could feel Tom at my shoulder all the way. He dipped when I dipped but I still got there first.

'Give me another 20 metres and I'll be past you,' he whined.

I smiled sweetly at him.

'Give me another 20 metres and I'll really be hitting my stride,' I replied.

'How was it, darling?' Mum asked when I got home.

'Pretty hard work,' I admitted. 'Tom was being Tomish, if you know what I mean.'

Mum nodded thoughtfully.

'You just stick to your guns,' she said. 'He'll get his comeuppance, if not on Sports Day then soon enough.'

That 'if not on Sports Day' comment worried me

at first, but then I pulled myself together and focused on what *was* under my control, which for the time being meant homework. I slogged through maths and geography before picking up what I really wanted to get on with: my Eric Liddell project. But as soon as I started, I realised that I was stuck.

'What's wrong, love?' Gran asked.

I was working at the sitting room table while she was reading some cheap thriller.

'Oh nothing really,' I replied. 'Just this school project. I've got to finish it off but I don't know when I can get back to the library.'

'What do you need to go to the library for?' Gran asked, folding back the page in her book.

'To find out what happened to Eric during the war,' I said. 'Like we discussed yesterday.'

It wasn't like Gran to be forgetful.

'Oh did we?' she said. 'It rings a vague bell. Well, I wouldn't bother if I were you. They sell off most of their stock these days, so you're probably better off buying whatever you need.'

'I want to look at some more original documents,' I said.

Gran considered this carefully.

'Why cut down trees when someone's already made a chair?' she said.

I had no idea what she was talking about. For once,

Gran realised as much.

'OK, I see I'm going to have to translate that for you. What I mean is why do the research yourself when someone else has already done the hard work for you?'

'What, use the internet, you mean?'

Gran picked up her book and started banging her head with it.

'No, that's absolutely not what I mean! What I mean is get yourself some biographies of Liddell. But don't bother checking whether the local library has them. There's no chance. You could try buying some online, I suppose, but that could get expensive. I reckon your best bet is contacting those two running buddies of yours. What are their names again?'

'Frankie and Olivia?'

'They're the ones. Frankie goes to some posh school, right? They're bound to have a decent library. And isn't Olivia's mum something big in the historical world?'

'Well, I could try,' I said doubtfully. It was true that Olivia's mum was a historian but I didn't know if she'd have any books about Eric Liddell, let alone be prepared to lend them.

'That you could,' Gran said. 'So stop sitting there looking gormless and get on with it.'

Which is why Mum caught me on my phone with Gran peering over my shoulder when I should have been doing my homework. Gran backed me up when I tried to explain but, to be honest, I'm not sure having her on my side always helps. It certainly didn't help when my phone started beeping while Mum was having a go at me. I was sorely tempted to sneak a look, but I thought that might be a red rag to a bull, so I waited until she was out of the room.

It was a text from Olivia. I have to hand it to her, she didn't hang about.

'No probs,' her text said, 'I'll sort it.'

That was good enough for me. I packed my stuff away, pecked Gran on the cheek and went up to bed.

The next two days I was so agitated waiting for the book to arrive that poor Alice really got the rough end of it. I stumbled over her Lego castle and sent it flying, then I trod on one of her dolls. It was all a bit of a disaster really.

In the end Mum sent me off for a run. It's the only way I can really clear my mind when I'm on edge because when I'm running all my worries disappear and I concentrate on just two things: the run and myself. Not what I've done or what I'm going to do, what I think or even what I feel, but the real me.

When I'm running it feels like the world has faded away. It feels like I'm ready for lift off. Running flat out but somehow accelerating as well.

I am the arms that are pumping. The legs that are striding out. The breath that is pulsing. When I'm running I don't have a body: I am my body.

There's nothing I enjoy more than getting up early, pulling on my running kit, and stepping out into the fresh, morning air. I love striding out across an empty park and getting a rhythm going. I love the dull ache in my legs after I've been for a run. It's a reminder that I've trained well.

But there's more to it than that. What I really love is running fast. The nervous tension before the start of the race. The exhilaration of bursting out of the blocks. The thrill of rounding the bend into the home straight. When I'm running fast, I know that my body and I are one. That sounds odd and I can't really explain it, but it feels really, really good. What I'm trying to say is that when I'm running, I am complete. When I'm running, I feel completely free.

So Mum was absolutely right to send me out on a run because when I got back in I felt a whole lot better. Then the postman turned up at the door with a bulky parcel. I tore open the brown paper and found three books and a note inside.

'Found these in our library,' it said. 'Mum said to borrow them for as long as you like. But don't lose them or sell them because at least one of them's rare and expensive, but I'm not telling you which one in case you get ideas. Love, Olivia.'

'You've got to hand it to these homeschoolers,' Dad

said admiringly, as he had a good look at what she'd sent, 'they certainly keep a good stock of books. Don't trust anyone else to resource you. I like that attitude.'

'Thanks, Dad,' I said, taking back the books. 'I'll look after these.'

I know what he's like. Give him a sniff of a book and he'll hide himself in a café somewhere and work his way through it, ignoring whatever else he's supposed to be doing. But I didn't have time for that. My project was due in a few days before Sports Day and the big day was now rapidly approaching.

When I got up to my room I had a proper look at the books. There was a biography of Eric Liddell, which is what I'd really been after, but Olivia had also sent a couple of books written by inmates in some Japanese prison camp. The first one was written by a monk of all people. 'This is one of my mum's favourite books,' Olivia had written on a post-it note which she'd stuck to the front. That sounded encouraging, so that's where I decided to start.

20

Eric
Weihsien, China, 1943

It is not every day you see a monk wading around in pools of human waste, but the first time I met Patrick Scanlan he was indeed knee-deep in excrement, so perhaps I should explain how we came to find ourselves in this strange situation.

From the moment the Japanese attacked the American fleet at Pearl Harbour we found ourselves in an impossible position. It may have been a day or two before Britain and the USA declared war on the Japanese aggressors and many months more before we were sent to the prisoner-of-war camp at Weihsien, but our fate was sealed the hour those bombs dropped.

We were the enemy and eventually the time came for us to be treated as such. We received orders to travel 400 miles to the Civilian Assembly Centre in Weihsien, which is what the Japanese called their prison camp. We took with us what we then thought was the bare minimum, being allowed only three cases. Most of us brought clothes and other essential items, but one man arrived with a set of golf clubs while another carried his cello.

I packed plates, cups, a blunt knife, a fork, my Bible, and some clothes, including my Edinburgh University blazer and my spiked running shoes. To my shame, I also packed curtains, for some reason that now escapes me. However, even they became useful. As the weeks turned to months in that terrible place, we cut them up to make shirts and trousers. I also brought some of my athletics medals, though I gave my Olympic Gold to Florence for safekeeping before she sailed to safety in Canada. They proved to be useful too, as I shall explain.

What we actually needed when we arrived were shovels and a strong constitution. With 1800 men, women and children packed into a compound designed for 200, our most pressing need was waste disposal. We had two latrines between us and no way of disposing of our waste. The smell was appalling and the risk to health even worse. If we wanted to stay healthy we had no choice but to plunge into that stinking mound of human excrement so we could unclog the sewers and create a system that would cope with the strain we placed upon it. We had no choice but we were still unwilling to dive into the filth. Forgive me for this description—I am unused to writing about such matters.

There were few volunteers for that terrible job, so

you can imagine my surprise when a group of Roman Catholic monks plunged in where the rest of us feared to tread. Hitching their robes up above their knees, they attacked the thick brown mulch with makeshift shovels. Heaving it into some buckets we had begged from the guards, they passed it from hand to hand before dumping it into a trench outside the camp walls. It goes without saying that the Japanese guards kept a very close eye on them, but it also goes without saying that they kept their distance too.

No one worked harder than Patrick Scanlan, a Trappist monk who had lived a life of almost total silence before the war. But now he was in his element. As he dug he sang in Latin, cracked jokes in English, and roared with laughter whenever any of his fellow monks slipped and took a ducking. He was not at all what I had imagined a monk might be.

He and I soon became close friends and allies, because I quickly discovered that he had another great skill: he was a wonderful smuggler. He told me that with my athletics medals he would be able to buy eggs, tomatoes, watermelons and a great deal more besides because he had made contact with nearby Chinese villagers and persuaded them to trade with us, their food for our precious possessions. I willingly handed over the medals, though I must admit that I was glad that I never had to choose between my Olympic Gold and food.

Under cover of darkness Scanlan broke into an drain and crawled through the foul sewer until he reached the iron bars at the other end. There, outside the camp's heavily fortified walls, he met terrified Chinese villagers who offered him their goods at hugely inflated prices. They were desperately poor and we were desperately hungry, so we did not object.

If the goods were small enough to fit through the bars, they pushed them through. If they were not, they simply flung them over the wall. On one memorable occasion, we bought a goose and were surprised to see that it was still alive when the villagers threw it into the camp. It hit the ground and promptly ran off down the street until one of the prisoners managed to smother it with his pyjamas and wring its neck before the guards realised what was happening.

My job was to assist Scanlan in distributing the contraband food around the camp. Hiding eggs, jam and vegetables inside our clothes, we took it to those who needed it most, though none of us did a better job than Scanlan himself.

I wondered why he continued to wear his monk's robes when his work often coated him in dirt and excrement, but I soon discovered that there is no better place to hide smuggled goods. His scapular (a kind of cloak that covers the shoulders and the top of the chest) was especially useful. I never ceased to be amazed by the number of eggs, tomatoes and even chickens he could conceal under it.

Of course, the Japanese often caught him, even though the other monks acted as lookouts, but somehow he always managed to drop the goods he was smuggling before they laid hands on him. Without any evidence, there was little the guards could do.

Then, one day, his luck ran out and he was caught with fourteen tins of jam and a packet of sugar under his robes. The Japanese sentenced him to two weeks' solitary confinement, forgetting that he was a monk, and a Trappist at that, for whom two weeks alone with the Lord is more pleasure than punishment! He sang his way through his time in that cell, sometimes in Latin and sometimes in English. Ten days of this was enough for the guards. When they could no longer stand his cheerful songs of praise, they released him and demanded that he behave himself in future. Which, of course, he did not.

Then, one day he came to see me with terrible news. He and most of the other monks were going to be transferred out of the camp. I do not know where he went or why he was ordered to leave, but I do know that our lives became poorer and hungrier without him. As soon as we heard the news, we all knew that we would miss him desperately. That is why so many of us lined up to pay our respects and to see him and the other monks off. Of course, the guards forced us back but, as Scanlan was marched through the gates, he caught sight of me and waved a hand in greeting.

'*All shall be well*,' he shouted, '*and all shall be well, and all manner of thing shall be well.*'

I did not know what he meant but I hoped that he was right.

22

Lili

'I know we are all very much looking forward to Sports Day,' the headmaster announced at assembly.

'Speak for yourself,' Mollie Davis muttered from behind me.

'And a very special Sports Day it's going to be this year,' he continued, smiling beatifically in my direction.

I kept my head down.

'With the big event only ten days away...' he said, before breaking off and correcting himself. 'With Her Majesty's visit only ten days away, perhaps now is the time to remind you all of a few basic rules and regulations. First, full school sports uniform is to be worn at all times. Second, timing is crucial, so make sure you are where you are supposed to be in very good time. And C, remember it's the taking part that counts, not the winning.'

He carried on for some time about not asking the Queen for a selfie, but I kind of zoned out. As did most of the school. There was so much shuffling I'm surprised we didn't wear holes in our seats. He only got our attention back when he demonstrated how we should curtsy if were lucky enough to be introduced to Her Majesty.

'What was that all about?' Tom asked, as we walked out.

I was taken aback. He didn't normally talk to me. He talked *at* me quite a lot, but actually asking a question that required an answer was pretty much unheard of.

'The head's pep talk, you mean?'

'Just that bit in the middle,' he said. 'All that guff about it's just taking part that counts. Give me a break! I'm running to win. Which, by the way, is exactly what I'm going to do.'

'I wouldn't be too sure about that,' came a voice from behind me.

I turned round to see who my unexpected supporter was and saw Mohammad Siddiq. I gave him a grateful nod of acknowledgement.

'I reckon Harry's going to knock you into third place.'

'Third!' Tom was incredulous.

'Yeah,' Mohammad smirked. 'I'm going to win by a mile. And as for Lili, she's going to be lucky to make the top six.'

Tom punched him.

'You're an idiot, Mo,' he said, 'but you got one thing right: who ever heard of a Chinese sprinter?'

I kept smiling at them both but inside I felt terrible. There was enough pressure hanging on the race itself, especially with the Queen there to watch it, without me having to deal with them constantly harping on about China.

Sophie must have realised that I was a bit down because she nabbed me at break and force fed me a snack-size tub of Pringles.

'OK,' she said, once we'd polished off the whole tub, 'what's the problem?'

I sighed.

'What do you think's the problem?' I replied. 'Tom's the problem.'

'Tom's always the problem,' Sophie said, 'so that can't be the real problem. And don't look at me like that: you know what I mean.'

I grinned because it hadn't made a lot of sense.

'Tom is the problem,' I said, 'but now Mohammad is the problem too. They're both having a go at me.'

Sophie snorted.

'Of course they are,' she said, 'because they're terrified you're going to show them up on Sports Day.'

'But why do they have to go on and on about me being Chinese?'

'Because they're looking for a way to wear you down, that's why. They don't care about China or Scotland or England, or anywhere else for that matter. They only care about themselves. That's why they're lashing out at you.'

'But I do!' I said.

'You do what?'

'I care about China and Scotland and England. I love China because it's where I'm from. I love Scotland because it's where Mum's from. And I love England because it's where I live. But I love them all but in slightly different ways.'

'So…'

But I interrupted Sophie before she had a chance to say any more. I was on a roll now.

'I love our country, terrible weather and all, because it's our country, but I love China because it's right inside me, so far inside me that I can't always put my finger on it. It's part of who I am. So, when those two give me a hard time about it, it really hurts.'

'I know,' Sophie said quietly, 'so what you've got to do is stay strong, keep training, and then run them off the track on Sports Day. That's the only thing that'll shut them up.'

And then she threw her Pringles tub straight into the bin from about ten metres. If she ever gives up sprinting she should really take up the javelin.

The bell went before we could talk about it any more, so I spent all of French mulling over what she'd said. The great thing about French is that it's one of those lessons where you can get away with not doing very much as long as you put on a thoughtful expression.

So, I set my face to thoughtful and then tried to calm

myself down. Once I'd done that, I realised that Sophie was probably right. There's wasn't any point in fighting fire with fire. The only language Tom and Mohammad would understand was on the track.

And then I realised something else. The two of them had really hurt me by going on and on about China, but they'd really annoyed me too. Deep down I was fuming and sometimes anger can be stronger than pain. I knew that I couldn't let them beat me. I knew that I had to win. And somehow I knew that I was going to win. It was a great feeling.

'*Merci, Madame,*' I said with a big smile at the end of class. 'I really enjoyed that class.'

Madame Aupetit looked confused and then pleased. I suppose no one had ever said that about a lesson on the subjunctive before.

'That's so nice of you to say,' she replied. 'Maybe we can carry on with the *subjonctif* next time.'

Sophie prodded me in the back before I could agree and then hissed at me when we were just about out of earshot.

'What was that all about?' she demanded.

'Oh nothing,' I said happily. 'It's just that I know what I need to do now.'

'About time too,' she said. 'Now I can get on with my own preparations without having to worry about you all the time.'

'Oh, and one more thing.'

'Yes?' she said wearily.

'Don't you love the way she says *subjonctif*?'

We both laughed and the tension was broken.

When I got home I gave Mum a big hug to her great surprise and then wrote out a list of Chinese sprinters, which I stuck to my wall before I went to bed. I'm not sure I really needed to but it certainly made me feel better. This is what it looked like:

Chen Kingkwan

Chen Yinglang

Chi Cheng

Ge Manqi

Li Airu

Li Sen

Liang Xiaojing

Liu Changchun

Liu Ping

Liu Xiang

Mo Youxue

Poh Kimseng

Su Bingtian

Tang Pui Wah

Tao Yujia

Leonard Tay

Wei Yongli

Xie Wenjun
Xie Zhenye
C K Yang
Yang Chuanguang
Yu Xiwei
Yuan Yu Fang
Zhang Peimeng

Mum stuck her head in while I was writing but, when she saw what I was doing, she backed out again. Dad would have blundered in and talked away at me and Gran would have made some wildly inappropriate comment, but Mum always knows when she needs to keep quiet. That's one of the things I love about her. And that's why I let her correct my list when she came in to kiss me goodnight.

'It's a good list,' she said, 'but you've missed off one name. Can I borrow your pen?'

I nodded and watched as she added a name in her best handwriting. Then she kissed me again and tucked me into bed.

It was only when she'd gone that I picked up my phone and looked at what she'd written:

Number 25—Lili DeLisle.

23

Eric
Weihsien, China, 1944

It was the children who troubled me the most. With only boredom and hunger to fill their time, they were quickly becoming wild. Charging through the camp, they tormented prisoners and guards alike while most of the adults slumped in their bunks and did their best to ignore them. What those children needed was a guiding hand and a listening ear, so I attempted to provide both. And when I listened I realised that their greatest need was an activity to keep them occupied. That is why we organised our athletics competitions.

Those competitions breathed life into the whole camp because the adults wanted to be involved as much as the children. My own training was fitful to say the least but I raced every time, for there was always someone who wanted to beat an Olympic champion. One of the doctors suggested that I should allow a child to beat me for the sake of morale, but I gently refused because I did not want to give anyone an opportunity to boast. I ran to win and that is what I did, even when I grew weaker with lack of food. I also insisted that the children should run to win because we should always give of our best. In the same way I encouraged them to play to win in their games of hockey, though I also insisted that they play by the rules. They needed discipline as much as they needed determination.

There are many, even today, who badly misunderstand discipline. It is the guarantee of peace, order and happiness. Without it we stumble and fall. Where would the Christian be without discipline? Where the athlete? Neither could possibly reach the goal set before them. That is why we established rules in the camp, not to keep people in their place but to set them free.

Nonetheless, one of these rules proved too heavy a burden. Every Saturday evening I locked the room where our meagre sports equipment was stored—footballs, hockey sticks and the like. I unlocked it again on Monday morning because the Sabbath was a day for the Lord, not a day for games. For many months such an arrangement was accepted without question, but one day I returned to the store to find that the lock had been forced.

After further investigations, I discovered that some of the more rowdy boys had broken into the store and borrowed the hockey equipment so they could play an impromptu game on Sunday afternoon. Without a referee, the match had descended into chaos. Punches were thrown and hockey sticks were used as clubs, resulting in several black eyes and a few bruised egos. I fixed the lock but my heart was troubled. The children knew the value I placed on observing the Sabbath, but in the extreme conditions of the prison camp even this eternal rule seemed fit to be challenged. I prayed late that night and pondered what the good Lord would have me do.

24

Lili

I couldn't decide how to approach the final training session: whether to really go for it to psych Tom out completely or to take it easy and preserve my energy for Sports Day itself. In the end Billy made the decision for me.

'There'll be no races this afternoon,' he announced at the start of the session. 'No silly mind games and certainly no physical contact. Today's a day for stretching and limbering up, followed by some work on your technique. And, frankly, some of you still need it, before anyone thinks about complaining.'

Nobody did. I guess we all had our minds on the race itself.

There was nothing else that afternoon but the race. In fact, there'd been nothing else all term. It was the thought that dominated all others. 12 seconds or so. Over in a flash. And yet so much hung on it.

The whole season had been leading up to this point. The day we had all been training for coming to a head in one short burst of controlled energy. One race. *The* race.

Nothing else came near it.

I guess that's why that particular training session remains something of a blur. At least, that's one reason why it's a blur. I guess we must have done lots of stretches, but I can't remember which ones. I suppose we must have done some work on our technique, but I've no recollection of it. The afternoon was a wipe out.

I do remember the final lap though, a slow warm down which I did with Sophie. We jogged round the track together in companionable silence while the boys ran ahead, hurling insults and trying to trip each other up. It was good to have a friend I could rely on, a friend I didn't need to say anything to. She understood how I was feeling and that was enough for me.

'OK, everyone, that's it for the evening. Good luck on Thursday and say hello to the Queen from me,' Billy said when we got to the finish line. He never went in for open displays of emotion. But as I walked across to pick up my trackie top, he strolled over for a final word.

'You've got it in you to beat him, Lili,' he said. 'Him and all the others too. Don't let me down.'

I gulped back the lump in my throat and nodded. Then he clumped me on the back.

'But it's not about me,' he added. 'Just do what you know you can do and you'll be all right.'

I nodded again, attempted to flash him a thankful smile and rushed off to join Sophie. She was standing outside the changing rooms and she was talking to someone. A teacher, I thought at first. But then I gave a start because it wasn't a teacher at all: it was Mum.

Perhaps I haven't mentioned Mum enough. I guess I haven't because she's such a rock-solid part of my life that I don't have to. It's really Mum who holds the whole family together. Dad's a bit all over the place and Gran's borderline crazy, so we need someone who's able to keep us all under control. And Mum's definitely got us where she wants us. She hasn't worked since we adopted Alice—"Hasn't worked for money," she always corrects me—but, even so, she's never pampered me either. She never takes me to school for a start. Or collects me afterwards, for that matter. If I'm late then I'm late, and I have to deal with the consequences. She reckons I can stand on my own two feet. So there's no way she was going to pick me up after school when there's a perfectly adequate bus stop quarter of a mile down our road. That's why I was so surprised to see her talking to Sophie outside the changing rooms.

'Mum!' I shouted, breaking into a delighted run.

Then I saw the expression on her face.

'Mum, what's wrong?' I shouted, suddenly anxious.

'Lili!' she called back, holding out her arms for a hug.

We briefly embraced and then I tried again.

'Mum, what is it?' I asked. 'Why are you here?'

She looked down at me and didn't let go.

'It's your Gran,' she said. 'She's been taken ill and she's had to go to hospital.'

It had been a light training session and I had scarcely raised a sweat, but suddenly I felt my heart pounding as though I'd run the 200 metres flat out.

'We've got to get there straightaway.'

═══════════════

The hospital they'd taken Gran to was a soulless place, full of long corridors and chipped walls. Everywhere we looked we saw anxious relatives and stressed out nurses. There wasn't a doctor in sight. Gran was in Intensive Care, hooked up to all sorts of machines that beeped away like a bunch of phones someone was trying to ignore. I've always thought of hospitals as quiet places, but the room Gran was in was incredibly noisy. After only a few minutes the beeping really started to get on my nerves. But we weren't in there for a few minutes: we were there for hours. I wondered how Gran could possibly bear it.

Gran herself seemed to have disappeared under a mass of wires and tubes. I tried to trace them back to a machine, like those trails you get in puzzle books, but there were some that got away from me. However hard I tried to follow them, they seemed to get tangled with other wires or tubes and then turn back towards

Gran, who was lying horribly still with her eyes closed underneath them all.

'She's had a stroke,' Mum whispered, 'and they think there might be a problem with her brain. They're going to run some scans.'

I nodded again, not trusting my ability to speak.

I took Mum's hand and squeezed it hard, then looked at Dad who had Alice in his lap. She seemed completely baffled by what was going on and so did Dad. As I looked at him, I noticed that he was crying. I'd never seen him cry before and I didn't like it. Then I realised that I was crying too and I didn't like that either. I buried my head in Mum's jumper and let myself go while she stroked my hair.

'It'll be OK,' she said. 'One way or the other, it'll be OK. The doctors know what they're doing and she's in the best place for her right now.'

I reached out to give Gran a stroke, but she didn't respond at all. I know it sounds an odd thing to say about someone in her nineties but she looked really old.

'Come on,' Mum said once we'd stayed there a while. 'We need to get you some food.'

'But...' I protested.

'Dad'll wait here while we eat. And eat you must because you're going to be no use to Gran or anyone else unless you do.'

It made sense when she put it like that and suddenly I

did feel really hungry, not having eaten for at least eight hours. I stifled my protest and let her take me to the café. By the time we got there, Alice was asleep, so I ate my Spaghetti Bolognese while Mum cradled her in her arms and munched on a Mars Bar. It didn't seem much of a supper, but for once she didn't mind.

As we walked back to Gran's room, I tried to convince myself that everything was going to be OK, that she would have woken up, that the nurses would be waiting to tell us that she could go home, but of course it wasn't like that. She hadn't stirred. There wasn't the slightest sign that she was going to recover consciousness. The only thing that had changed was that Dad had moved his chair closer to her bed and was holding her hand. He looked up as we walked in and smiled.

'Take the girls home, Anne. I'll stay here.'

'But—' I started to protest.

'You need your sleep,' Dad interrupted, 'and so does Gran. Don't worry: I'll look after her here and we'll see you again in the morning.'

25

Eric
Weihsien, China, 1944

I felt terribly weary this morning. In fact, I feel weary all the time now due to the inadequate diet and the pressure we are under. I am used to being tired—every athlete is—but this is different. It is a tiredness that seems to come from within, a terrible lethargy that it is impossible to shake off. I would fight it off if I could but, as I can't, I must accept it and battle on. The race is not to the swift nor the battle to the strong, I must always keep that in mind.

Yesterday the camp's disciplinary committee made a decision for the greater good of the camp. We will open the sports equipment store every day, though only after the midday meal on the Sabbath, so all those who wish to can still attend a Sunday service. It is a decision I regret but accept. Maybe that is why I feel so weary.

I attended our service this morning and handed all my worries to the Lord. Then, after a meagre lunch, I trudged over to our store, where I found an orderly queue of children already waiting outside.

I handed over a ball and as many hockey sticks as I could lay my hands on, but the children did not rush off to the field. Instead they held back, as if waiting for me to say something.

'Who will be your referee?' I asked, as much to encourage them to move as to get an answer.

Since the only answer I received was a resigned shrug of the shoulders, I realised that I had to make a decision. For years I have endured mockery and ridicule for my refusal to play sport on the Lord's Day, but now, in a Japanese prison camp in North-Eastern China, I had to make my decision all over again. The children looked up, strangely patient as they waited for me to speak.

'What shall we do, Uncle Eric?' a little lad asked.

That is what they call me here: Uncle Eric. Offering up the situation to the Lord, I knew that I had to respond as an uncle, not as a preacher.

'I will be your referee,' I said, 'if it will stop you beating each other black and blue.'

And so it was decided. Today, for the first time in my life, I took part in a sports fixture on the Sabbath and I believe the Almighty looked down on our little match with joy. Certainly he granted us a charitable peace for it was the best-tempered game I ever oversaw.

'Will you help us again next Sunday?' one of the boys asked, as we collected the hockey sticks at the end.

'Maybe,' I said. 'But first we have the camp athletics competition. I trust you are all going to compete next Saturday?'

From the cheers and whoops of delight, I gathered that they would all be there.

'What about you, Uncle Eric? Will you be running?'

Knowing that I was wholly unfit to compete, I looked down at the children and smiled.

'Of course,' I said, 'I wouldn't miss it for the world.'

26

Lili

We spent the next three days in hospital. That is, we stayed there in relays. Dad stayed a night, then Mum stayed a night, and during the day we all tried to be there, though Mum insisted on getting us outside every now and again, not for exercise but to stop Alice going stir crazy.

And not just Alice, I guess. We were all feeling pretty cooped up in that terrible hospital ward. We all needed to get outside to free ourselves from the intensity of the wait. We started by walking round the hospital garden but there's only so long that could keep us going. Dad suggested that we go to some woods that were just down the road, but nobody wanted to be far from the hospital, just in case.

Just in case. It was a phrase that dangled there, unwanted. I tried to brush it away but it kept swinging back in front of me.

'Why don't you go for a run?' Mum suggested. 'Just a short one around the hospital grounds. I've slung your running gear in the boot of the car.'

142

But, for once, I didn't feel like running. It didn't seem right somehow. Not with Gran lying there unable to move.

'Maybe you ought to...' Dad began, before Mum shushed him.

I wondered why and then I remembered the race. It had dominated my thoughts for weeks and yet the shock of Gran's illness had driven it completely from my mind. *You've got to get your preparation just right*, Billy had told me. Well, this wasn't the preparation he had in mind. I tried to think about Tom and wondered what he would be doing now. Not sitting in a hospital waiting room, that was for sure. He'd be doing his exercises or going through his starting block routine or trying to out-psych Mohammad.

I tried to get myself worked up about it, but I just couldn't. Now that Gran was in hospital, running down a track seemed trivial. Unimportant. Irrelevant.

And yet... And yet there was a part of me that couldn't let go. I'd been running for so long, training for so long, preparing for so long. Running was what I did. Running was who I was. It wasn't a habit I could shake off just like that.

It was in my body as much as it was in my head. My legs were calling out for a good stretch. My arms missed the drive out of the starting blocks. My lungs needed to breathe deeper than they could in any hospital. I decided to go outside so I could think straight. I needed some time on my own.

The first time I visited Olivia's house she showed me how to catch a chicken. You can't just dive in. You can't run up to them head on. You have to creep up on them from the side. 'Obliquely' was the word Olivia used. That's the way Mum approaches any sensitive conversation. She leaves me for a while, then she gently introduces what she wants to say from the side.

But Dad's not like that at all: he just dives in. When I walked back into the ward, he plunged straight in with his question. 'Obliquely' is not a word in his vocabulary.

'So are you going to run in this race or not?' he said.

I still didn't know. The walk hadn't really helped.

That's what I told Dad, hoping he would let the subject drop. But there was no chance, of course. He was like a dog with a bone.

'You must have some idea,' he said unhelpfully.

I just shrugged.

'OK, so it's like that, is it? Well, perhaps I'd better help you out then.'

He took Gran's hand.

'What do you think Gran would want you to do?' he asked.

That was the question. What would Gran want me to do? I just didn't know. She certainly didn't let illness or injury get in the way of everyday life. Not in the usual course of things anyway. I remember visiting her house when I was young. When we got there she was halfway up a ladder with a broom in her hand, trying to dislodge some obstruction from the guttering.

'Do you think you should be doing that at your age?' Mum had asked.

It was the sort of question that always drove Gran up the wall.

'At my age?' she had replied indignantly. Then she winced, put her hand to her chest, dropped the broom, and almost fell off the ladder. 'Oops,' she said.

We talked her down eventually but she wasn't happy.

'Oh do stop fussing!' she complained as we made her a soothing cup of tea. 'It was just a little wobble, a little bit of fun. I really don't know what you're all going on about.'

'We're going on about the fact that you're 87 years old and you almost fell off a ladder,' Mum said.

Gran waved the worry away with a dismissive shake of the hand.

'When I actually fall off a ladder you can fuss,' she said. 'Until then, you can relax. Oh, and if you don't mind clearing your suitcases out of the hall, I'd be most grateful. I was thinking of doing my monthly hoover this afternoon.'

Mum groaned but did as she was told, taking Dad with her. Gran then took Alice on her lap and poured another cup of tea.

'The thing is,' she confessed when they were out of the room, 'I did fall off the ladder a couple of days ago but I wouldn't be telling them that.'

I tried not to look too worried.

'Did you break anything?' I asked.

'Oh, only a couple of flower pots,' Gran replied breezily, 'and one rib, but that's to be expected. I do throw myself around a bit.'

That's the sort of woman she is. *Can Do* personified. Nothing stops her when she's made a decision to do it. Somehow I couldn't see her allowing a hospital stay to get in the way of the race of the season.

But, on the other hand, I know how much she loves her family. Her family and everyone else's. She loves spending time with us and she loves us spending time with her. And now here she was laid up in a hospital bed for the first time in her life. What would she want me to do? Carry on regardless? Stick around until she had fully recovered? Stay with her in case she didn't recover? I just didn't know.

'Lili?' Dad said quietly, interrupting my thoughts.

'I'm not sure, Dad,' I said. 'I…'

But as I started talking, I realised that I had already reached a decision. The biggest decision of my short life.

I had been training all season for this race. Beating Tom had become an all-consuming passion. Every spare second had been devoted to getting ready for Sports Day. This was the race that mattered. The race the Queen would be watching.

But actually it didn't matter. Not really. Not in comparison with being with Gran when she needed me. Running is important. It will always be part of me, part of what I do and part of who I am. But it isn't life itself. Some things are more important. People are more important. Gran's definitely more important.

'I'm going to stay here,' I said quietly. 'There will be other races but Gran needs me now. She needs us all now.'

Dad looked at me with a broader smile than I had ever seen from him before, and I felt a huge weight drop from my shoulders.

'That's my girl,' he said.

27

Eric
Weihsien, China, 1944

The whole camp was there for our athletics meeting. There was little to do in our prison, so any distraction was welcome, and this meeting was more than just a distraction. It was a major event.

Paul's words to Timothy ran through my head as I prepared myself: 'I have fought the good fight, I have completed the race, I have kept the faith.' I knew all about fighting and faith, but completing the race was another thing altogether. I didn't know if I had the strength for it any more.

My running kit had long gone. I had traded it for food or given it to someone whose need was greater than mine, I forget which.

I still have my spikes but they are now the shoes I wear around the camp, every other pair having been worn to pieces. I sometimes think I should have given them away too because some of my fellow prisoners have no shoes at all but make do with strips of cloth wrapped around their bloody feet. We are all in a pitiful state.

I pushed myself through a warm up routine that used to come as easily as breathing but now, after months in the camp, I can no longer complete it without breaking into a raucous cough. I stretched and pain shot up though my body. I tried to touch my toes and got nowhere near. I jogged and my body felt as heavy as ten-ton weight.

I knew, though I told no one, that this would be my final race. If truth be told, I knew that I was too weak to manage even this race. Nonetheless, I had to honour my commitment to the children. They were all expecting me to run. They were all expecting me to win. For their sake I would compete to the best of my ability. For their sake I would push through the pain as I had pushed through pain a thousand times before.

If my last race was to take place in a Japanese prison camp then at least I had the consolation of knowing that I would never have a more appreciative crowd. The world had changed but the people who really mattered had not. I would run for China and I would run for Scotland too. I would run for the children, my family, and God. I would run for them all and know that the heavenly hosts were cheering me on.

The track was the same as it had always been. Starting in the field, we headed out into Main Street, across Market Street and Tin Pan Alley before arriving back at the field but, because we were so weak, the organisers limited the race to two laps rather then the customary four. That was a relief to us all.

As the starter climbed onto a packing case, I tried to compose myself but it was difficult. The sun was beating down, the guards' dogs were growling, and my body was already begging for a rest. However, there was nothing for it but to run. The starter waved his handkerchief to send us on our way and I sprang into action.

I ran that race as I ran the Olympic final twenty years before. I knew that if I could establish a lead I was unlikely to be caught because my kick was so much stronger than anyone else's. The others knew what to expect and formed a chasing group behind me, with young Aubrey Grandon leading the pack.

I ran as hard as I have ever done in my life, and as I ran I seemed to see all the races I have ever run, all the matches I have ever played. I remembered school rugby matches and university competitions. I remembered my first cap for Scotland and my final match too. I remembered racing on uneven tracks in Scottish fields and I remembered running in the Olympic stadium in Paris. I will never forget that day. The surge of pace from the starting blocks. Rounding the first bend with no sign of anyone breathing down my neck. Entering the back straight with the roar of the crowd behind me. And then the final bend and the realisation that I was still out in front. I remember pushing, pushing, pushing, my head going back, and the relief and wonder of breaking through the finishing tape in first place.

And then I was back in the present. I could hear the children cheering and the guard dogs barking. As we reached Tin Pan Alley for the last time, I also felt a presence at my back. It was Grandon and he seemed to be gaining in strength. I strained for the extra pace that has always come so easily but no extra pace came. I tried to kick on but there was no power on which to draw.

Then Grandon surged past me and I knew that the race was lost.

28

Lili

And so our days acquired a new pattern. We stayed with Gran in shifts and ate at the hospital canteen. Mum spoke to school and persuaded them that it was all right for me to take a bit of time off, though that didn't stop them sending me work to do. But I couldn't concentrate on maths or geography or science. In fact, the only work that captured my interest in the slightest was my unfinished project on Eric Liddell and even that didn't seem so important any more. I did my best. I re-read Olivia's books while sitting in a chair next to Gran's bed. Then I tried writing up what I'd learned while sitting in the same place. It meant my handwriting was all over the place, but that didn't seem to matter too much either.

I wrote about Eric's time in the camp, about the hockey match he refereed and about his last race. I wrote about the time he gave his running shoes to another prisoner who was hobbling round the camp in only a pair of socks. I wrote about the mystery illness that got worse and worse until even Eric admitted that he had to go the camp hospital. And then I wrote about the brain tumour that killed him, though it was a bit of a struggle to get that bit down on paper.

In fact, that was what I was working on when an unexpected visitor turned up. Sophie had popped in a few times and both Olivia and Frankie had sent flowers. My class at school had made a card, which was unexpectedly sweet of them, though I noticed that neither Tom nor Andy had signed it. In Andy's case, it was probably because he couldn't spell his own name.

So you can imagine my surprise when Tom wandered in, a bunch of grapes in his hands.

'I thought your Gran might want these,' he said, thrusting them at me like they were about to explode.

'Oh right,' I said, completely gobsmacked.

Neither of us knew what to say, so we stood there in silence for a minute. The only thought that went through my head was that he'd come all this way to crow about winning the 100 metres at Sports Day. I feel bad about that now.

'So how did Sports Day go?' I asked in the end, as much to break the silence as anything.

Tom scratched his nose.

'Yeah, it was all right. Mohammad won and I came second. Sophie beat Harry into fourth place. He wasn't happy about that.'

I smiled for what felt like the first time in weeks.

'I bet he didn't,' I said.

And then we stood in silence for a bit longer.

'And the Queen?' I added. 'Did she show up?'

'Yeah, she was there. She said we all did very well.'

'Was that it?' I asked.

Tom scratched his head and then absentmindedly ate one of the grapes.

'Yeah, that was about it,' he added. 'You didn't miss much.'

He scratched his head again and glanced over at Gran.

'She had a big hat.'

I grinned. If that was all he could come up with, it was probably best to let him go. Catching him by surprise, I gave him a quick hug. I've never seen anyone look more shocked.

'Yeah, right, I'd better get back to school. It's rugby training and, well, you know…' He trailed off. 'Maybe next year.'

I must have looked confused because he added: 'Maybe next year we can have that race after all. You know, when your Gran's better.'

It was as close as Tom ever got to showing some sort of human emotion, but it meant more than any long speech would have done. I almost gave him another hug. A great big one this time. But I didn't. It wouldn't have gone down well.

'Yes, maybe,' I said.

He turned to go.

'Thanks for coming,' I added. 'I appreciate it.'

''S'all right,' he muttered without looking back, and with that he was gone.

And then I didn't know what to do. I stood there for a while longer and then I went and gave Gran a kiss on the forehead. After that I picked up my project and carried on writing. There was something I wanted to get down, a little detail that somehow seemed very important.

In 1945, several months after Eric's death, Florence received a parcel in the post. Inside were Eric's few belongings, including a piece of paper he'd written on on the day he died. He'd been copying out a couple of hymns, *Abide With Me* and *Be Still, My Soul*, but in the top left-hand corner he'd written another little phrase: '*All will be well.*'

I looked over at Gran. Her eyes were closed, her chest was gently rising and falling, and there were wires all over the place, but she looked peaceful. I took her hand as I thought about Eric, China's first Olympic gold medallist. He may have lost his last race in that Japanese prison camp, but I reckon he won the race that really mattered. I gave Gran's hand a gentle stroke.

'All will be well,' I whispered and then I kissed her again.

THE END

Author's Note

When I was a young child, I loved sport, but as I grew older rugby knocked the stuffing out of me and swimming lessons finished me off, so I started to skive PE and threw myself into books instead. However, when I moved to the Lake District for my first job, I rediscovered my lost passion. I joined the local football, cricket and hockey clubs and, finding that I was pretty quick on my feet, tracked down the local athletics club too.

Running soon became a major part of my life. I trained on a windswept track on Walney Island and competed across Lancashire and Cumbria. I loved running fast. There was nothing better than rounding the bend in the 200 metres and knowing that I was running full pelt.

I started off as a sprinter, then became a distance runner, then gradually stopped running competitively, though every now and again I'd pull on my trainers and rekindle my athletic passion. It was on one of these occasions, when I was out running with my eldest daughter, that the opening words of this book hurdled into my head. I took the idea and ran with it.

By this time, I had become intrigued by the story of Eric Liddell. *Chariots of Fire*, which told the story of his Olympic success, was a great movie but I was fascinated by his life after the Olympics. It was a great untold story and so I resolved to tell it.

At first I thought that *The Race* was going to be Eric's story alone, but then Lili rounded the bend at top speed. The more I wrote, the clearer it became that there were two runners in this race and so my novel became a dual narrative.

It also became quickly apparent that, like Eric, Lili would have to be both Chinese and British. Her history mattered just as much as his did. And the reason I felt so strongly about that is because my own family is multi-national. More specifically, it has been immeasurably enriched by the adoption of my two precious children, so I wanted to bring something of that wonderful experience into my book. I wanted to tell a story about adoption that was both realistic and positive.

But, of course, as any writer will tell you, there's only so much control you can exercise over your own book. Eventually the story, if it's good enough, will run away with you. And that's what happened with The Race: I fired the starting gun and then watched in amazement as it ran down the track.

So now that we've all reached the finishing line, I hope that you too have been swept up into the excitement of the race. I hope that, as you round the final bend, you too have known the joy of running fast and free.

Acknowledgements

I am extremely grateful for all the help I have received while writing this book. I must start with Anne Glennie, who gave *The Race* a chance to compete in the first place. Anne is a remarkable person: publisher, editor, designer… Are there any limits to what she can do? It's been a real delight to join Clan Cranachan, so I'd also like to thank all my fellow Cranachan authors for their warm welcome and encouragement.

I am also grateful to the staff at SOAS, University of London for their help as I tracked down material about Eric Liddell. It was such a great privilege to hold his letters from China in my hands, to pour through boxes of his belongings, and to immerse myself in his world. And, just to be absolutely clear about this, the SOAS librarians never once told me to keep quiet or threatened to throw me out. They were helpfulness personified.

I would also like to thank Shaunagh Brown, Sally Magnusson, and Allan Wells for reading the book in advance and for commenting so generously on it. I am in awe of them all and so am extremely grateful for their time and kindness.

My greatest debt of gratitude, as always, is to my extraordinarily patient family, especially my wonderful wife and daughters. Like sprinting, writing is a solitary pursuit that can only be done with the support of a great team, and team Peachey is the best one out there.

About the Author

Roy lives with his wife, two daughters, two dogs, two cats, one rabbit, one tortoise, and a few fish. When he isn't spending time with his family, writing books, or looking after the menagerie, Roy is a teacher.

Peachey's first novel for adults, *Between Darkness and Light*, the story of a translator with the Chinese Labour Corps during World War I, was published in 2019 by Eyrie Press. He is also the author of four non-fiction books: *Popes, Emperors, and Elephants*; *Out of the Classroom and Into the World*; *50 Books for Life*; and *Did Jesus Go To School?*

roypeachey.com
@roy_peachey